If you want to get the measure of a man, you have to understand where he came from, know his roots, and find out what made him into who he is.

Don't be fooled by my humility and down-to-earth charm. I grew up in the lap of luxury. I had the perfect childhood, surrounded by loving relatives and all the material things a child could want. There were times when I felt guilty for my good fortune, but hey, that's the luck of the draw.

By 1996 I was a strapping lad of fourteen, attending a prestigious school in Johannesburg. I was smart, popular, and good at almost everything. My teachers told me I was a prodigy...

...Or they would have, if they hadn't been so busy trying to discipline me. Okay, so maybe it wasn't exactly the lap of luxury. Maybe it was a hard-knock life in the township, but it had its moments. Perspective, I've realised, is everything. There were glory days, even for an orphaned kasi kid. And on one particular day, my whole world changed.

I remember every magical detail. Rubbish heaps towered high near the school yard and the wind blew scraps of litter around us. The more athletic kids played soccer on our second-class pitch, kicking up clouds of dust on the bare ground as they chased their makeshift ball. The loiterers lingered in the dim corridor, breathing in the priceless scent of rubbish and sweat.

The smart kids (like me) had more important pursuits to focus on. I made my way down the corridor, weaving between the loiterers. I was a man on a mission. Under one arm I carried an old leather-bound book. I found my best friend Vusi sitting close to the soccer pitch, watching the game with wide eyes like it was the World Cup. He was kind of chubby, in that cute way that made people want to pinch his cheeks. He wore glasses, too. Not a great look when you're fourteen and dying for a little street cred.

I dropped the book on the floor next to him to get his attention. He jumped, startled, then turned around and picked up the book.

"What's this, Senzo?" he asked, in the calm, no-nonsense tone I had come to know so well. It was the tone he used when he sensed that I was about to reveal one of my brilliant ideas.

You see, even in my youth I prided myself on honesty, hard work and integrity. I figured a kid as bright as me had a responsibility to use that intelligence to serve the greater good and establish myself as a role model in the community.

I grinned, winked and sat on the floor beside him. "This, Vusi, is our latest scam."

"An... An-tho-lo-gy of Twen-ti-eth Cen-tury Po-e-try?"

I shook my head, disappointed. "We must work on our reading, Vus. We must practice until we sound like TV presenters."

He glanced at me. "Where did you get this book?"

"The library."

"How?"

"Borrowed it."

"Didn't they ban you after you started selling their books?"

I shrugged. It was just like Vusi to dwell on the details and miss the bigger picture. I really needed to find a way to stop him from nit-picking.

"Check this out," I said, taking the book back. "Next week we start English poetry. I got the list of poems we'll be doing and –"

"How?"

"Never mind. I..."

"Did you steal it?"

There it was again. Nit-picking.

"Ag, stop judging me and listen!"

Vusi snorted, but didn't say another word.

"Most of the poems are in this book," I explained. "And they have essays and study guides. All we have to do is offer to do people's essays for them. How much do you think we should charge? I'm thinking ten rand a pop."

He glared at me.

"Fifteen rand?"

He sighed. "Senzo, we'll get busted."

"Me, I say if you believe, you will achieve."

He snatched the book. "We *always* get busted."

"Always? What always? We have a seventy percent success rate!" I snatched the book back. "And when it's time to write our own poems, we just copy them from the list at the back. How much do you want to bet Mrs Mahlangu won't even check?"

Vusi didn't reply. His expression told me he was one hundred per cent opposed to my master plan, but I wasn't about to let him rain on my parade. I was on a roll, already mentally spending our hard-earned cash.

"For originals I'm thinking twenty rand each, hey? What do you say?"

He couldn't have looked less impressed if he tried. "This is the dumbest plan you've come up with so far."

"It's fool proof," I assured him.

"Please. No one's going to fall for –"

"Hey, poet!"

We both turned towards the sound of the belligerent voice. One of the football players was running towards us. Jasper Ndlovu, aka Idiot Extraordinaire. He was in our class, one year older than us and a whole lot bigger. But you know what they say. The bigger they are, the harder they fall.

He stopped in front of us, scowling at me. "Where's that poem you promised me? My girl is ready –"

"No deposit, no poem," I interrupted.

"Eh?" He wasn't used to small fry like me talking back, but I liked living dangerously.

"I told you, as soon as you pay the deposit, you'll get the poem. Don't you understand English? De-po-sit."

Jasper took one step towards me, cracking his knuckles. "That's it. I'm going to do this for your own good since you don't have parents to teach you manners."

I smiled. "Ja, maybe your mother can –"

Before I could finish my sentence, Jasper lunged. Vusi leapt between us, always the peacemaker, and then pointed toward the gate.

"Whoa, whoa, whoa. Guys, look!"

A mini-van taxi had just pulled into the school yard. The doors opened and out stepped the most unlikely passenger – a middle-aged white lady. I don't mean those ones who like to hang out in the townships with their black friends, either. I'm talking smart shoes, expensive clothes, hair in a tight bun and a determined smile combined with wide, panicked eyes. She looked around her. Her smile faded a little, then she plastered it back on like a pro and turned towards the other passengers in the taxi.

That was when I noticed that the taxi was full of people who definitely didn't belong here, and I remembered the TRC initiative our school was participating in. Truth and reconciliation, my foot. Those people didn't look reconciled, they look terrified. The woman stood aside as the kids spilled out of the taxi, one white face after another. They were about our age and dressed in the neat uniform of some snooty school in the suburbs. Me, Jasper and Vusi stared. Another white face. Another white face. And then...

The last person to emerge from the taxi was a girl. A black girl. The most beautiful girl I had ever seen.

The teacher's voice carried over to us as she directed her class across the yard, but I couldn't hear anything except the pounding of my own heart. The kids formed a line and marched obediently towards the classrooms.

"Oh my God, look how scared they are!" Vusi clicked his tongue in annoyance. "It's like they're visiting a zoo!"

Jasper and I stared at the goddess with the shy smile. I strained to catch a glimpse of her name tag as she and her classmates walked past us. Wait...yes! There it was. Ayanda Zwane. I mouthed the name silently as she swept past, committing it to memory. The name of my future wife. There was no doubt. It was love at first sight.

"Viva truth and reconciliation," I whispered, still gazing after Ayanda.

Jasper turned to snarl at me. "You'd better give me that love poem when we're in class, or I'll kill you."

Ja, ja, ja. I didn't even notice him strutting away. I was floating in a love bubble, and not even Jasper's obnoxious ways could ruin my mood.

*

By the time we were ready for our Truth and Reconciliation session, I was head over heels. I was vaguely aware of two people standing in front of the class – matronly Mrs Mahlangu and her slender pale-skinned counterpart, who was introduced as Ms McKenzie – but I struggled to focus on them. I didn't care that the small classroom had grown hot and stifling with the addition of nine white teenagers and their beautiful black queen. I couldn't pay attention to Vusi's jabbering ("Hey, check out that one looking at our desks like she's scared she's going to catch a disease!"). All I cared about was Ayanda.

I wasn't the only one. I soon noticed that Jasper was ogling her. The piece of scum didn't even have the decency to treat her like the gem she was; he gaped at her, practically salivating, like she was a steaming bunny chow he wanted to devour. I felt a powerful urge to leap from my seat to defend her honour, but I had the feeling that might not go down so well. After all, I didn't want her only memory of me to include a black eye.

With a sigh, I tore my gaze from her angelic face and tried to tune in to what was going on around me. Unburdened by the prejudices of our parents, we found it easy to mix amongst ourselves. We black kids mixed with our own on the far side of the room close to the window, while the white kids mixed with their own on the other side close to the door. We had, by some sort of telepathy, agreed to leave a nice even space between us. There. Integrated.

"Truth and reconciliation is about forgiveness," Mrs Mahlangu was saying.

My gaze strayed back to Ayanda. How was it possible for any teenager to have such flawless skin? I could imagine how it would feel to caress her cheek...

"Ja," said Ms McKenzie in a shrill voice, snapping me back to reality. "Ubuntu. Batho Pele! Amandla!"

I winced. Vusi snorted. Our classmates exchanged confused glances, and Mrs Mahlangu looked at the other woman out of the corner of her eye.

Ms McKenzie cleared her throat. "Why don't we all hold hands and say re-con-ci-li-at-tion together?"

"Good idea," said Mrs Mahlangu. "Everyone, holds hands with the person closest to you."

Good idea? *Good idea*? I couldn't think of anything more embarrassing. Then again... I looked at Ayanda. All I had to do was move one seat forward and I could take her hand. But someone else had the same idea, and he was faster. Jasper dived for Ayanda's hand. I shifted my seat, but it was too late. He was closer. The next few seconds seemed to happen in slow motion, like a scene in a movie. Jasper's hand stretched out and grasped. Ayanda hesitated, then held out her hand. I watched as Jasper's big, clumsy, unworthy fingers closed over Ayanda's lovely, delicate ones, and I wanted to howl.

Everyone started chanting "Re-con-ci-li-a-tion". I chanted along absentmindedly. While they were all going on and on about reconciliation, I was reconciling myself with my crush on Ayanda. Then, out of the corner of my eye, I saw Jasper staring at me. He let go of one of the hands he was holding – the one that wasn't Ayanda's, obviously – and drew his finger across his throat. What was he going on about? Oh, the poem!

I released Vusi's hand. He looked at me, but seemed a little relieved. I reached for my notebook, scribbled on one of the pages then ripped out the page, folded it and passed it on to Jasper. Just as I expected, he didn't bother opening it. My heart pounded as I watched him write "4 Ayanda frm Jasper" on it, then hand it to her. Obviously the girl he had initially intended the poem for had slipped his mind as soon as he clapped eyes on Ayanda. What a gentleman.

Ayanda's eyes widened as she took the note. I watched, holding my breath. She opened the note and read it. A few moments later she frowned, crumpled it up and tossed it right back in Jasper's face. I leaned back, satisfied. Mission accomplished.

Jasper had no idea what was going on. He picked up the paper, smoothed it out and read its contents. The expression on his face was priceless. I started to laugh, starting with a kind of snort and then a sound like hiccups. Soon I was wheezing so loud everyone turned around to stare.

"What in the world is going on over there?" Mrs Mahlangu demanded.

Jasper was too angry to respond, and I was too busy laughing.

"Jasper! Senzo! Stand up, both of you!"

I rose to my feet. The laughter had faded now that the class was quiet and all eyes were on me. I glanced at Jasper.

"You want to tell everyone what's so funny?" asked Mrs Mahlangu.

Jasper replied in Zulu. "Senzo is busy insulting – "

"English please," she interjected.

"Sorry, Ma'am." Jasper held up the note. "Senzo is busy writing insulting poems to people."

Mrs Mahlangu sighed. "You know the rules, Senzo. Come up here and share the poem with the class."

"But Ma'am –"

"Now, Senzo." She arched her eyebrows. "Or else."

I gulped. I knew exactly what that meant. Corporal punishment was alive and well in our school. I made my way to the front, picking up my notebook and snatching the crumpled paper from Jasper as I went. I shoved the page into my notebook, and once I reached the front of the class, I opened the book to the first page, cleared my throat and started to read. I still struggled with reading English, especially out loud. The words got stuck in my throat and I stumbled.

"There is so much I want to...share with you, but...but my words are lost with... within me –"

"That's not what he wrote!" cried Jasper.

"Quiet, Jasper!" said Mrs Mahlangu, with an embarrassed glance at Ms McKenzie. "Senzo, proceed."

I took the opportunity to start over. "There is so much I want to share with you, but my words are lost within me. I have so many em...emotions. How do I make you see?" I risked a glance at Ayanda. She, like everyone else, was watching me intently. I cleared my throat again. "Life is not that simple. Hear this from my heart. Our love will con...conquer all, as we stand here at...at... As we stand here at the start."

I looked up to gauge the reactions. Ms McKenzie gave me a dreamy look. I couldn't blame her; I was adorable and charming. Mrs Mahlangu didn't seem to know what to think. Vusi stared at me with his mouth open, flabbergasted by my hidden talent. Jasper looked unimpressed. Good. And Ayanda... Ayanda was smiling, and that was enough to give me wings. I carried on, fearless.

"Not speaking to you is killing me, you there and me here. But one day soon that will change, and I will finally have you near." Emboldened by her expression, I looked her right in the eye as I delivered the last line. "But now I stand here and wonder, if I will ever have you – Aya –" I broke off, suddenly too nervous to follow through.

A chorus of "Oooooohhh" went up around me, and for a second I wished everyone but Ayanda would disappear. I looked at her, waiting for her to give me a sign that she understood, and maybe felt the same way. She gave me a sign, but not the one I was hoping for. She looked away and buried her face in her hands. I felt all my bravado seep away and I got a funny ache in my chest, like someone had scooped out my heart.

"That was beautiful," gasped Ms McKenzie. "Such talent in the townships!"

Mrs Mahlangu wasn't so easily impressed. "Ayanda, you think your future husband can afford your lobola?" she teased.

My peers burst into laughter. The only person who might have been on my side, Vusi, had buried his head under a book. Jasper was having the time of his life, laughing his stupid head off. I ripped the page out of my notebook, flung it into the bin and ran out of there.

"Hey!" yelled Mrs Mahlangu. "Come back here!"

I ignored her. Stupid move. Later on, when Ayanda and her classmates had left, Mrs Mahlangu and her cane taught me a lesson. I walked towards the door afterwards, trying not to wince. The first person I saw when I stepped out into the sunlight was Jasper, cracking his knuckles.

"My turn," he said.

There was no time to prepare myself. What followed was sharp, searing pain, and then lights out.

*

The St. Martins Orphanage was the biggest building on the street. It had to be big – it housed over a hundred kids and was attached to a chapel and a small clinic. I grew up surrounded by other kids, many of whom were just as adventurous and, uh, *accomplished* as I was. We were raised by (mostly) pretty women who worked hard to teach us good values, we got three decent meals a day, had clothes on our backs and a roof over our heads, and when we were bad the worst we could expect was a bunch of prayers and an hour or two of cleaning. By kasi standards, we had it made.

Sure, there were days I wished I had a Nintendo Gameboy like that clown Jasper, or a TV, or trousers that fit instead of donations and hand-me-downs, or, you know, real proper parents, but for the most part I rolled with the punches. I was a survivor. Adapt or perish was my motto. And when things got really tough, I had my boy Vusi.

Vusi, who was nowhere to be found while I was getting up close and personal with Mrs Mahlangu's cane. The same Vusi who went off to play soccer while Jasper gave me a bloody nose to go with my sore bum. I didn't blame him. Vusi liked to stay out of trouble. I was the one who liked to go chasing trouble down the road, waving a red flag.

When I walked in through the gates of St. Martins that day, Sister Lucy was there, watering the flower pots.

"Hello Senzo," she said cheerfully. "How was school?"

I mumbled a vague reply and trudged past her.

Sister Lucy grabbed my arm and spun me around to face her. "Hey, wena. Manners first." She peered at me, taking in my war wounds, and when she spoke again her voice was softer. "Oh, Senzo! Did you get into trouble again?"

"No," I murmured.

"Tell me what happened. Was it that boy Jasper again?"

I pulled my arm out of her grip. "You're not my mother! Don't pretend you care." I started to storm away, but she grabbed me again.

"Look at me when I'm talking to you, Senzo."

I deliberately looked the other way, just to annoy her.

She sighed. "Me and all the other sisters may not be your family, but we love you and this is your home."

Home. Right. I gave her a questioning look. "What happens when I leave?"

She smiled. "You'll find someone else out there who will love you, even more than we do. You have to believe that, Senzo. Do you believe that?"

I considered for a second. My experience with love was rather limited. No parents, no relatives. I knew Sister Lucy cared, but love? That was something that happened to other people. I thought of the way Ayanda hid her face after I read my poem, and I felt a wave of humiliation come over me again. She didn't love me. No one loved me. Why would anyone love a no-good kasi orphan?

I walked away without a word, leaving Sister Lucy alone with her flowers.

2.

Life continued to shower me with blessings in the years that followed. That's what happens when you work hard, behave in an honourable fashion and live up to your full potential. You become a beacon of hope for the people around you. You become, like me, wildly successful.

Fifteen years after Ayanda stole my heart, I ran a thriving business in the heart of Johannesburg. My office was smack dab in the midst of the big city chaos – the cars, the smoke, the countless faces. I soaked it all up. My clients were among the wisest and most discerning people in the city, people who knew what they wanted and were happy to pay top dollar to get it. And I, of course, was happy to oblige.

My daily routine was what you would expect from a mogul. I woke up in my lavish apartment. If it had rained there might be a puddle in the middle of the bedroom floor, due to the artistic leaks in the roof. I would turn over on my old mattress – beds were so 1999 – and kiss my female companion awake. I had a way with the ladies. Something about my air of mystery and entrepreneurial spirit drove them crazy. I wouldn't call myself a chick magnet – but other people would.

On this particular day, however, I woke up alone. Sometimes a creative guy like me needs a little space to get his mojo back. I took a cold bath – I really needed to remember to talk to the landlord about that geyser – and walked across the room to shake Vusi awake. Yes, Vusi was still around. He was the only part of my old life that remained, the only person I could trust. I taught him everything I knew and shared my success – and my home – with him. That's what friends do. He hadn't changed much. He still had those thick glasses and now braces as well.

"Come on, Vusi, we're already late."

He grumbled, turned over and looked at the time on his phone. "Ag, Senzo, five more minutes."

I returned with a cup of cold water, which I dumped all over him. He jumped up, making me laugh. Even after all these years, he never saw it coming.

We arrived at our consulting room just in time to beat the morning rush. I suppose I should explain what I mean by "consulting room". Let me put it this way: people came to me with problems, and I made the problems go away. The biggest problem most of my clients had was what I like to call FEID Syndrome. That's Financial Excess and Intelligence Deficit, or as Vusi liked to say, money to burn and no clue how lighters work. That's where we came in. I was the match, Vusi was the flame and together we made magic happen. Just like old times.

Me and Vusi had come a long way since our school days. Maybe not in terms of education – we both got our matric but never bothered with varsity. But all those books I "borrowed" from the school library had paid off. We read and read and read, and practised all the big words until we could speak like professors. We used to sit in Vusi's house listening to the radio and copying all the different accents. The ability to switch seamlessly from tsotsi taal to upper crust English was essential in our line of work. We never knew what opportunities might come up, or who we'd have to be in order to make the best of them.

The consulting room had very specific decor. Skulls, beads, animal hides. There were also a couple of tortoise shells and a stuffed vulture for good measure. As soon as we had set up for the day, Vusi disappeared behind a thick black curtain and I put on my uniform – shades and a dreadlock wig – and took my spot on the reed mat on the floor.

About one minute before opening time, I started to rock back and forth and hum. It was delicate work, and I had to create exactly the right atmosphere. My consulting room was like a dentist's office. Everything people saw and heard was a little unnerving, but they went in anyway because they needed the good doctor to make the pain go away.

There was a soft rap on the door, and my first client walked in. I stopped humming long enough to welcome him in, take his money and offer him a seat on the mat. His expression told me he was intimidated, which was always a good sign.

"So you're Prophet Mazinga?"

"Yes indeed. What's your name, my son?" I asked in my best wise mage voice.

"Tshepo." He was dressed in an old tracksuit. Not exactly minting money, this one. "So is it true? Will you really make me hear the spirits talking?"

I carried on chanting a moment longer, then stopped suddenly and said, "Listen!"

Tshepo shut up and looked around him. I picked up the cup next to me and took a sip from it. I closed my eyes and let the spirit world take me. Or something.

"What is the name of your lover, Tshepo?"

He gulped. "It's...ah...Ayanda."

I spluttered, spilling the contents of the cup all over myself. The curtain behind Tshepo billowed slightly. Coincidence, I told myself, struggling to regain my composure. There were a lot of girls named Ayanda.

"What's wrong?" asked Tshepo.

I coughed. "Nothing. The spirits seem to be...confused. They're saying..." I started rocking and humming again.

Suddenly there was the sound of furtive whispers. I knew they came from behind the curtain, but Tshepo almost jumped out of his skin.

"Ayanda," the whispers called out. "Ayanda, Ayanda, A-yan-da..."

Tshepo let out an undignified shriek. "Oh my God! Oh my God! This is real!"

I raised a hand to silence him while the whispering continued.

"Ayanda... Ayanda will come back... if..."

Tshepo leapt to his feet. "If? If what?"

And then we all heard the unmistakeable sound of a cell phone ringing. I opened my eyes. Uh oh. The phone rang again. Tshepo looked at his phone. It was off. He glanced at my phone, beside me on the mat. It was also off. A muffled thud came from behind the curtain, and then a whispered "Shit!"

Tshepo turned around.

"My son, you must sit down and listen to what the spirits –"

It was too late. I'd lost him. Tshepo went to the curtain and pulled it aside. There, sitting on a stool and fumbling with his phone, was Vusi. He looked up, mortified. Tshepo whirled around to glare at me.

"What the hell is this?"

"This?" I laughed. "Ah. Yes. I can explain. You see, the spirits –"

"You're a fraud!" snapped Tshepo. "I want my money back."

"Why don't we sit down and talk this over – "

Tshepo held out his hand. "My money. Now!"

With a sigh I fished the cash out of my pocket and handed it over. Tshepo took it and left without a backward glance. I turned to Vusi.

He crumbled beneath the force of my withering stare. "I'm sorry! I thought it was on silent!"

"You thought?"

"Hey, everyone makes mistakes!"

Another day at the office. Like I said, wildly successful.

*

When I left the old neighbourhood, I had no intention of going back. There was no nostalgia, no missing the orphanage, no high school reunion. Vusi was different. He was always looking back, keeping tabs on our peers. He knew who was married with kids, who had turned out okay and who had been swallowed up by the hard life.

It was Vusi who told me that my old nemesis Jasper had made good, thanks to his father's connections. He was on the BEE track to fame and fortune, apparently. I seethed inside every time I imagined Jasper sitting in a fancy air-conditioned office. I may not have been top of my class, but Jasper made me look like a genius. How could he be out there living it up while I hustled on a daily basis? It just proved what I had always suspected – life was unfair.

Fortunately I never had to worry about crossing paths with Jasper again. High-powered corporate types weren't exactly my biggest clients. The only time I rubbed shoulders with such people was at the traffic lights.

Vusi and I had closed up shop to go do a little marketing. We stood at the traffic lights in our regular clothes, handing out flyers to pedestrians and waving them in the windows of passing cars. A silver Lexus pulled up and paused at the red light. The driver, some suit with manicured fingernails, was deep in conversation on his phone.

"I didn't say she refused. I said she didn't have a chance to say yes," he explained patiently. "That bloody waiter ruined the moment. But she will say yes. I got her a diamond so big she won't be able to lift her hand!"

I could tell by his tone that he was speaking to someone important. I walked up to the car window and held out a flyer. He ignored me.

"She'll come around." He laughed nervously. "You know how women are; she just needs some time to think. Talk to her friends. Maybe pray about it."

I rolled my eyes and wriggled the flyer in front of him. He continued to ignore me.

"Just a few more weeks... Yes, I understand, but...eh...."

Fed up with his rudeness, I shoved the flyer through the window, right in his face.

"What's your problem?" he snapped, acknowledging me for the first time. "Can't you see that I'm on the phone?"

"Sure thing, bra," I replied casually.

He snatched the flyer and carried on with his conversation. "Yes Chairman, I understand. I will make sure that it gets done. I promise."

What a stuck-up snob. These black diamonds got a little taste of the good life and thought they were better than everyone else. I shook my head and moved on to the next car.

13

*

Vusi and I were very different people. I guess we had always been that way. I was the brilliant mastermind and he was the reluctant sidekick. I was the one breaking the rules and he was the one trying to keep me from getting caught. Most of the time it worked.

Everything about his life was more stable than mine. He was raised by his grandmother, so he had family. From the first time we met I could tell the difference between him and the orphans. There was a kind of certainty with kids who grew up knowing who they were and where they came from, even if the situation was tough. They were solid, steady on their feet. Steadier than the rest of us, anyway.

I suppose that's why we connected so well. We balanced each other out. So while I was off chasing girls, searching for something I could never find, Vusi was almost married. Technically Zanele wasn't his wife – he couldn't afford the lobola yet – but they had been together so long they might as well be hitched.

Zanele wasn't a fan of our operation. She wasn't thrilled about our living arrangements either, but since she shared a tiny flat with three other girls, she was in no position to do anything about it.

"Baby, we need a plan," she said that night, as the three of us sat in our usual shebeen, drinking away our sorrows.

"We have a plan," said Vusi. "We're saving."

"Ja, like ten rand a month," said Zanele. "We'll be dead before we can get married! You need a real job. Both of you," she added, glancing in my direction.

I'd heard this speech a thousand times. Get a real job, Senzo, everyone told me. With what, the first-class degree I got from the University of Nowherestad? What Zanele meant was that I should be a sucker like her, slaving away in a blue collar job to line someone else's pockets, while I struggled to make ends meet for the rest of my life. No thanks. I had no intention of giving up my calling to become a car guard in a shopping centre.

"It's complicated, baby," said Vusi softly, but I could tell by the way he shifted in his seat that it was only a matter of time before he caved. What was it about long-term relationships that turned men into mush?

"What's so complicated about it?" Zanele clicked her tongue. "You remember how you were almost arrested last time? Is that what you want?"

"No, but..."

"But nothing. The guys at my office are hiring right now. You should apply."

I chuckled into my beer. "You want Vusi to be a cleaner? I don't think the uniform would suit him."

Zanele gave me the dirtiest look she could manage. "Don't be stupid. The security company is hiring." She turned her gaze on her boyfriend and put on a coaxing lovey-dovey voice. "It's a good job, my darling. The uniform is smart, all navy blue. And we'll be in the same building, we can see each other all the time..."

I watched Vusi's expression go from doubtful to intrigued. Damn, she was good.

"Just think about it," she whispered, and then excused herself to go and primp.

"Forget it," I told Vusi as soon as the vixen was out of earshot. "You don't want to be a security guard. We want to be rich, remember? That's the plan."

"We're not getting rich, Senzo."

Ah, Vusi. Always the pessimist. "Not yet, but these things take time."

He gave me a look. "You've been saying that for years. This Prophet Mazinga thing was supposed to be temporary, and we've been doing it for almost two years now. And the scam before that –"

"Ja, okay," I cut in irritably. "I get it. You want to ditch me and go play house with your wifey."

"I'm not ditching you. I just think we need to, you know...think about things."

I looked up to see that Zanele was on her way back. I wasn't in the mood for another lecture, so I got to my feet.

"And now?" asked Vusi. "Come on, don't be angry."

"I'm not angry." I drained my beer bottle and left the empty on the table. "I'm giving you lovebirds some private time."

I walked away before Zanele reached our table, and stopped to say bye to Big Mama. She was the woman who ran the shebeen and she was tougher than any of the guys in there. No one messed with Big Mama. Everyone respected her. If she liked you she could be the sweetest, warmest person in the world. I was one of the lucky few. In fact I was her favourite, and we had a bond that went way back.

"I'm leaving," I told her, leaning over the counter.

She looked up from polishing the counter. "Good. You drink too much, Senzo."

I smiled. "I drink less than Vusi."

"I don't worry about Vusi. I worry about you." She looked at me. "You're a smart boy. You should do something with your life."

It was strange, but I didn't mind the lecture that much when it came from Big Mama. She wasn't just being a pain like Zanele. Big Mama was looking out for me. She always had. I had lost count of the number of times she had stepped in to save me from getting my butt kicked in a drunken brawl, or given me great advice. She had worked hard to build a little empire for herself, so I knew her advice was worth taking. But me being me, I didn't always listen.

"Something like what, Big Mama?"

She shrugged her plump shoulders. "Use your brains, boy. That's why you have them."

I laughed. "Goodnight."

"And stay away from that girl, asseblief."

"Which girl?"

Big Mama just raised her eyebrows. I waved and moved towards the door.

"Hey, Senzo," said a familiar husky voice.

Ah. *That* girl. I had a history with the owner of that voice, the kind of history that involved a lot of steamy drunken nights followed by sober mornings filled with regret.

I turned around with a sigh. "Hi, Sweets."

Sweets was a working girl, and hot stuff by kasi standards – tight dress, high heels, too much make up. But now, several months after our fling, I couldn't remember what I'd seen in her.

"Shame, you look lonely," she cooed. "What's up?" Her mouth was smiling but her eyes were cold. They say hell hath no fury like a woman scorned, and Sweets was proof.

"I'm fine," I told her. "I'm just going for a walk."

"You should be careful out there, hey. The streets aren't safe." She leaned close and whispered, "Not even for a prophet." Then she walked away, swinging her hips as if to show me what I was missing.

I shook my head. So far Sweets had kept her mouth shut about the scam, but I knew one day she'd find a way to use it against me. I turned away from her and stepped out into the night air. She was right; I was lonely. I always knew that Vusi would get tired of the wild life we led and want to settle down, but I didn't think it would be so soon. We weren't even thirty yet! The worst part was that he had a point. We had been running cons since high school and we were still broke. One way or another, we had to find a better way to make a living.

*

The next morning I went to work alone. Zanele had slept over, so I left her and Vusi and made my way to the consulting room. Everything was intact when I arrived, so clearly Tshepo hadn't bothered reporting us.

I had barely started setting up when I got a call from a prospective client. As soon as I hung up I called Vusi.

"I'm here, I'm here," he gasped, bursting into the room. "Why didn't you wake me up?"

"Man, I'm still traumatised from the last time I walked in on you and Zanele," I reminded him.

"Oh." He chuckled. "Ja."

"Why are you just standing there?" I asked, tugging my wig over my head. I brushed dust off the mat and sat down, then put on my glasses. "The client will be here any second!"

A knock on the door made us both jump.

Vusi dashed behind the curtain, then stuck out his head and whispered, "What's the case?"

"Standard Bring Back Lost Lover," I whispered back. I cleared my throat and called out in my gruff prophet voice, "Come in!"

A man entered. He was well-dressed, and the minute I saw him I knew he was going to be the professional highlight of the month.

I beamed at him. "Welcome, sir. Please take a seat."

He looked around as though he expected rats to come crawling out from the shadows. Reluctantly, he lowered himself onto the mat. It took him a few moments to find a comfortable position.

"Please relax," I told him, trying not to laugh. "Make yourself at home."

He grunted, then raised his head and looked at me. I realised he was the snob in the flashy car, the one who had been so rude to me at the traffic lights the day before! Ah, it made sense now. The girl he had spoken about on the phone, the one for whom he had bought the "diamond so big she wouldn't be able to lift her hand", was the lover he was trying to win back. Despite his cocky attitude and money, he still needed the help of a prophet to get the girl to marry him. What an idiot. If I played my cards right, we could make a killing from this fool.

"So, you mentioned your lover on the phone," I began. "What happened?"

He threw another wary glance around the room. "I proposed to her yesterday. It was perfect, you know. I took her to a very expensive restaurant, ordered the best champagne, got her a huge ring and everything. But halfway through the proposal the waiter showed up." He clicked his tongue. "Stupid bloody fool ruined the moment, and of course I lost my temper. Who wouldn't? But my girl is one of those sensitive types," he added impatiently, rolling his eyes. "She got upset when I shouted at the waiter, and she walked out. She's still not answering my calls."

I thought it was a miracle he could keep a sensitive woman with his attitude, but I kept that opinion to myself and instead nodded sagely. "Ah, I see, I see. And you want me to help you get her back?"

"Isn't that what you do?" He reached into his pocket and produced a folded piece of paper. He opened it and waved it at me. It was the flyer I had given him. "Prophet Mazinga from Mozambique," it read. "Penis Enlargement. See your enemies in a mirror. Bring Back Lost Lover."

I nodded. "I can help you. What is the name of your beloved?"

"Ayanda."

I couldn't resist a smile. Another one? That name was far too common.

"What's so funny?" the client asked.

"Nothing. Surname?"

"Zwane."

I froze. "Eh, excuse me?"

"Zwa-ne," he repeated.

I could still see her face as she stepped out of the taxi all those years ago. Ayanda Zwane. My first love. My only love, to be honest. One coincidence I could handle, but this? What were the chances that there was another girl in Joburg with the same name and surname? I took a deep breath.

The man leaned forward. "What's wrong?"

"Do you have a photo?"

He took his cell phone out of his pocket, sought the photo and handed the phone to me. As soon as I saw the photograph, I knew it was her. She was even more beautiful now, but she still had that sweet, shy smile and flawless skin. Ayanda. And she was dating this stupid, puffed up... I looked at the client again and a terrible thought occurred to me.

"Uh, what did you say your name was?" I asked.

"Jasper," he said, and my worst fears were confirmed. "Jasper N-"

"Ndlovu," I whispered. Oh my God.

"Hey! How did you know that?"

I looked into his obnoxious face and wondered how I'd missed it. Of course it was Jasper. He was bigger, more muscular and far better dressed than before, but he had the same smug face. Vusi had told me he was a bigshot, and now he planned to marry Ayanda. *My* Ayanda! History was repeating itself. Fifteen years ago he had enlisted my help to write her a poem, and now he wanted my help again. I would help him, sure. I would help him the same way I helped him before, and I would take as much of his money as I could in the process.

I sunk lower on the mat and pushed up my shades, just in case he recognised me. "Where did you meet this Ayanda?"

"I work for her father. But we first met in –"

"School?"

Jasper frowned. "How did you know?"

I smiled. "I'm good at what I do. Do you love her?"

"Of course. We have been together for the past year and a half, on and off."

"So why doesn't she want to marry you? Does she love you?"

"Of course she does. But that's beside the point. I'm paying you to get her back. Can you or can't you?"

I took a minute to gather my thoughts. I would have to take a chance here, but it would be worth it. "I'm going to need a little bit more time on this case. It seems to be quite complicated. I will need as much information as possible on this...Ayanda. What is her home address?"

"Blue Hills Estate. Number two-three-nine."

I pulled out my phone and typed in the information, my heart racing. "Work address?"

"Amazi Spring Water. 136 Caroline Street. We both work there."

I typed as fast as I could. "Where does she spend her free time?"

"Is all this information really necessary?"

I sighed impatiently. "Do you want her back or not?" Raising my voice to a shout, I added, "Do you doubt my powers? The ancestors say that it's a complicated case!"

And right on cue, Vusi did his part. "Ayanda...Ayanda...Ayanda..."

Jasper jumped. "What was that?"

I glared at him. "There are powers at work here, my friend. Powers." I leaned in menacingly. "What does she do in her free time?"

"Charity work," he blurted out nervously. "Um, at the St. Martins Orphanage, and some other places. An old age home, I think. And a legal clinic somewhere in Soweto."

I hesitated for a second before typing. St. Martins? Ah, there were too many blasts from the past coming back to haunt me that day. First Jasper and Ayanda, and now the orphanage. Maybe it was a sign. Maybe this was the job that would set me and Vusi up once and for all.

I nodded firmly. "Right, Mr Ndlovu, I need a deposit before I can begin my work."

"What?"

I looked him up and down. "De-po-sit. Don't you understand English?"

Jasper frowned and leaned closer. "Have we met before? I feel like I know you from somewhere."

I pushed my shades up once more and leaned away from him. "That's because I visit you in your dreams every night. I am the voice of tomorrow and the echo of yesterday. I am the painter of your destiny and the voice of your wildest dreams. And I can be your worst nightmare...if you don't pay your deposit."

Jasper reached reluctantly into his wallet and pulled out a wad of cash. I took the money and counted it out. Yes, it would do nicely. For starters.

"The ancestors thank you," I told him. "I will get started immediately. Did you sign up for the SMS updates? Just visit our website and fill in the contact form. SMSs are charged at one rand fifty. Look, is that the time already?" I got to my feet. Jasper followed suit and I ushered him towards the door. "Time for my next appointment. Good bye. And good luck. Not that you need it when you've got me on the case. Heh heh."

He paused at the door. "Are you sure this is going to work?"

Oh, for goodness sake. I put on my best air of injured mystique. "My son, if the ancestors sense doubt then it will not work. I will need that photo on your phone, by the way. Send it to the number on the flyer."

Jasper took out his phone and sent the picture. A moment later, my phone beeped.

"Thank you, my son," I said, patting his muscular shoulder. "Until next time."

He stepped out and I banged the door shut behind him. The second the door closed, Vusi emerged from behind the curtain and rushed at me.

"What the hell do you think you're doing? Are you crazy?"

I stared at the picture on my phone of Ayanda and Jasper cuddling. I covered Jasper's face with my thumb. Ah. That was better.

"You can't do this, Senzo. You know the rules. No personal jobs."

"This isn't personal. It's business. I have a chance to get even with Jasper after all these years, and I'm taking it."

"Like hell," hissed Vusi. "This is about Ayanda! You're still in love with her."

I wasn't listening. I was staring at her gorgeous face, imagining what it would be like to see her in the flesh again.

"How exactly do you see this playing out?"

"I think you're overreacting, Vus." I turned to face him. "Jasper is rich and stupid, and we need money. If we pull this off, we can make more than we've made in the last two years, and then we can get out of the con game for good."

He looked sceptical. "I've heard that before."

I held out the wad of money Jasper had left. "Look at this."

His eyes boggled when he saw how much money was in my hand, and then he shook his head. "If this was really just business, I'd say go for it. But it's not. Look how you're staring at her photo! You're going to get us caught. Why are you lying to yourself, bra?"

I glanced at the photo and sighed. "Fine. You're right. This is about Ayanda. Vusi, we have to get her back."

"We?" he croaked. "Who's we? Besides, you never had her in the first place."

I shrugged. "Minor detail."

Vusi let out an exasperated groan. "Okay, Mr. Minor Detail, how are you going to get her back?

I drew myself up to my full height and took a deep breath. "I have no idea."

3.

The most important part of any con job is research. It's not glamorous or exciting, but it's necessary. You have to know your victim – uh, client – inside out. You have to know who he is, where he comes from and what buttons to push to get what you want. This job came with a bonus, because in addition to doing my homework on Jasper, I also had to read up on Ayanda.

The day after my first session with Jasper, Vusi and I went to an internet cafe to do a little digging. It turned out that my beloved came from a prominent family. Her father, Gideon Zwane, was a multimillionaire. That's right – multi. He made his fortune when he found a natural spring on his farm. Being a smart businessman, he saw the potential immediately and Amazi Spring Water was born. Not that I was interested in his money. It was Jasper's money I was after.

Vusi whistled as he scrolled down the page. "Looks like lots of companies want to buy him out, but he's not selling."

"Uh huh." I was scrolling through the company website, searching for Ayanda's photo on the staff page. Ah, there it was, right under the title "Legal Division". She was a lawyer! Beauty and brains. My heart jumped. Was it all in my head, or did she get more beautiful each time I saw her?

"Wife deceased. Only surviving heir is his daughter," Vusi went on.

"Mmhmm," I murmured. I was now going through Ayanda's social media profiles. "She's incredible," I sighed. "Look at all the charity work she does! And she's a brilliant lawyer, and she runs marathons." I whistled, taking in her detailed CV. "She was on the debate team in varsity, involved in about a hundred extracurricular activities, always in leadership positions..."

"She sounds like a handful."

"Hey, when you're rolling with the top dogs you have to keep up," I replied, annoyed by his tone. "You don't understand how tough it is for a woman to make it in a man's world."

Vusi glanced at me. "What?"

I pointed at an essay she had written for a women's magazine. " 'Raised by a single father who was always at the office, and living in a mostly-white area, I knew that only one thing would allow me to compete on an even playing field. I had to be the best.' " I shook my head. "She's a superhero." I opened up the Amazi Spring Water website again and copied the company's contact details into my phone.

22

Vusi rolled his eyes and returned to his screen. "Hey, Amazi Spring Water is hosting a fundraising dinner event at the Galwegian Estates."

I leaned over to see. "It's on Saturday. Good. That gives us enough time to prepare."

"Prepare for what? We're not going to get Ayanda and Jasper back together, and she's obviously too good for you."

I gave him a dirty look. "You're free on Saturday, right?"

"No, actually I was..." He paused as my implication sunk in. "What? No way. You can't be serious, man. How the hell are we going to get into an event like this? Have you seen the price of the tickets? We could live on that money for a month!" He shook his head in his typical pessimistic fashion. "We don't even have the right clothes."

Vusi, Vusi, Vusi, always nit-picking. "Leave it to me. Have I ever let you down?"

He thought about it for a second longer than necessary. "Yes."

"Ag, come on." I slapped the back of his head and he winced. "Everything's going to go according to plan."

"Oh, now you have a plan?" he scoffed, following me out of the cafe.

"Yes. It's brilliant."

"Your plans are always brilliant, and yet they never work."

"Seventy per cent success rate, Vus," I reminded him. "Trust me, it's going to work. But first we need to do more research."

For the next hour we paid very close attention to Ayanda's life. Well, I paid close attention and Vusi called me a psycho stalker. The point is we learned some important things about the love of my life.

The woman didn't have a paranoid bone in her body. She was open and warm on social media, as if her thousands of followers were actually friends rather than random strangers who yearned to be touched by her angelic glow. She shared photos of herself at work, at the orphanage, out with friends. She was confident and hardworking.

She was also the sweetest person in the world. Her followers adored her. She posted cute uplifting messages and insightful articles. She spent her time trying to make the world better. Obviously we were meant for each other. With my big ideas and her big heart, we could change the world.

Ayanda clearly didn't believe in solitude. She was always surrounded by people. Everywhere she went she was accompanied by colleagues or friends. I learned from her social media that her entourage was made up of three people: Precious, Thandeka and

Mandla. One of them seemed be at her side at all times, usually Mandla. I got the impression, from the photos, that he was the gay best friend. Either that or he was really into pink.

Finally I logged out and stood up. "We need to do a little field work," I told Vusi with a wink.

"What does that mean?" He followed me out of the cafe.

I looked up and down the street, then crossed over towards the taxi stop. Okay, so I didn't exactly have a plan. I had the skeleton of a plan. Well, more like part of the skeleton of a plan, but it was better than nothing. After all, this time I had serious motivation – Ayanda. To have the chance to finally win her heart, I would have to devise the best plot of my career.

As we walked, I whipped out my phone and dialled. When someone picked up, I put on one of my tried and tested voices – Number 7, the Impatient Tycoon. "Hello? Amazi Spring Water? Look, I need to get hold of Jasper Ndlovu right away." I rolled my r's just enough to show that I had lived abroad. I grinned at Vusi. He looked dubious, as usual. "What do you mean he's in a meeting? He was supposed to meet me an hour ago!"

"I'm so sorry, sir," the secretary said, sounding flustered. "Let me check his schedule, maybe there was a mix-up."

I gave her a minute to check. Vusi nudged me, and I held up one hand to silence him.

"I'm sorry, but he only had two meetings scheduled for today," the secretary said after a moment. "The next one is for two p.m."

"Where? I'll try and catch him. He'd better have a good excuse."

She hesitated. "I can't give out that kind of information."

"Are you joking?" I shouted. A few passers-by turned around to stare at me. "What kind of outfit are you people running? The man made an appointment with me, I cleared my schedule, and he didn't bother to pitch up! He didn't even have the decency to call to cancel! If this is the way you do business, I have to seriously reconsider my investment! In all my years working in this city, I've never –"

"The Protea Hotel," she blurted out. "He'll be at the Protea Hotel."

Jackpot. "Pat yourself on the back, my dear," I said in my haughtiest tone. "You might have just salvaged a very profitable partnership."

I hung up and turned to Vusi just as a taxi screeched to a stop beside us.

"What was all that about?" he asked warily. "Where are we going?"

"We're going to Sandton to check up on our buddy Jasper. We need to know everything we can about our competition."

"You mean *your* competition." He climbed into the taxi after me.

I shrugged. "Minor detail."

*

"You know that this is crazy, right?" Vusi sank low in his seat in the hotel lobby. "Stalking people is against the law."

"We're not stalking him." I peered over the edge of the chair, scanning the lobby. "We're observing his movements."

"He's late anyway." Vusi glanced at his phone, then popped up for a peek. "It's already three minutes past two."

At that moment I spotted Jasper. His tall frame and broad shoulders made him hard to miss. He entered the hotel with a short man in his late forties, an Alfred Ntombela type.

"Nope, he's right on time," I whispered. "Doesn't that man look familiar?"

"Ja, he looks like the guy that's going to get us thrown out of here when he realises we're spying on him."

"Don't be so paranoid." I waited until Jasper and his companion had their backs to us, then I leapt to my feet. "Come on!"

The older man walked briskly, like every minute of his time was worth a million rand, and Jasper hurried to keep up. They were deep in discussion, but I couldn't hear what they were saying. I had to get closer.

Someone up there must have been on my side, because at that moment the older man suddenly yanked Jasper's ear. Jasper yelped.

"You did what?" the man bellowed.

"You said to use whatever means necessary, Chairman," Jasper countered, rubbing his ear. "And I had to act fast. It'll work, I assure you. I hear he's very experienced in –"

"How do you think I became one of Africa's leading businessmen?" Chairman interjected.

Jasper hesitated. "By bribing your way to the top?"

"Yes! I mean no! By being ruthless." The man took a menacing step towards Jasper, and even though Jasper was twice his size, I could tell that my old nemesis was scared. Chairman whispered something I couldn't hear. It must have been a threat, because Jasper's eyes widened and he nodded meekly.

What was going on? Was Chairman just another business partner, or was Jasper mixed up in some interesting extracurricular activities? They continued to speak in hushed tones. I strained to hear, and at one point I was almost certain I heard Jasper say Ayanda's name. What did she have to do with anything? I inched closer.

"And you'd better stop bringing those other girls to your place," said Chairman.

Jasper laughed. "But I'm a red-blooded man, Chairman. I have needs."

Huh. I knew it. Jasper had been a player in school and it was no surprise that he hadn't changed.

"I'm not saying stop, I'm saying find a new playground," the older man replied. "If you screw this up because you can't keep your trousers on..."

"Understood," said Jasper nervously. "I'll be careful."

I had to find out what those two were plotting. But first I'd need more resources. I pulled out my phone, ducked behind a pot plant and called Jasper. His phone rang shrilly in the lobby and he stopped to answer it.

"Let me take this quickly," he said.

Chairman just kept walking.

"Yes, why don't you go ahead and I'll meet you at our table?" Jasper called after him. "I'll be right there." Poor guy, trying so hard to pretend that he was in control, when it was obvious he was nothing more than a puppet on a string.

I looked at Vusi and held a finger up to my lips. Jasper's voice came over the line.

"What do you want? I'm busy."

I shook my head. "Is that any way to talk to your prophet?"

Jasper sighed. "Fine, I'm sorry. What can I do for you, Prophet?"

"This case is very complicated," I told him. "We're going to need more time. And money."

"How much?"

I arched my eyebrows at Vusi. He shrugged. I fumbled for a number and picked the first one that popped into my head. "Twenty thousand rand."

Jasper coughed and spluttered. "Are you out of your mind? Where am I supposed to get that kind of money?"

"Do you want your lover back or not?"

There was a brief silence. I stole a glance from behind the pot plant. Jasper was pacing the floor nervously. Good, let him sweat.

"Look, I'm very busy and it will take a while –"

"Maybe you can borrow from one of your other girlfriends," I suggested.

Jasper froze. Jackpot. "How soon do you need it?"

"Transfer it into my account. I'll SMS the details. I'll resume working as soon as the money clears. By the way, when will you see Ayanda again? At the office?"

"No, I won't be going back to the office today. But we're having dinner with her father tomorrow night to celebrate his birthday."

"Which restaurant?" I demanded.

Jasper hesitated. "You're not going to show up there, are you?"

"Do you want my help or not?"

He sighed. "I'll send you the address."

I hung up and sneaked another peek at him. Chairman had entered the hotel restaurant, leaving Jasper standing alone in the lobby. I grinned at Vusi, then sent Jasper my banking details. A moment later he responded with directions to the restaurant.

"This is definitely the worst idea you've ever had," said Vusi.

"You always say that." I turned away from Jasper and moved towards the hotel entrance.

And just at that moment, Ayanda walked in. I was so shocked by her presence that I shoved Vusi to one side, flattening both of us against the wall so she wouldn't see us.

"Mmhhmmngg!" said Vusi.

"Ssshhhh!"

I watched Ayanda walk across the floor, graceful like a gazelle in the savannah, or something. She was dressed in a black skirt that showed off her gorgeous figure, a grey shirt and high heels. She walked like a model, confident, beautiful...did I say beautiful already? She carried one of those huge fancy handbags that women like, the ones big enough to hold a small person. I wondered what I would find if I got my hands on that bag.

"Unnnnngphhh!" said Vusi.

I watched Ayanda until she vanished into the restaurant. What was she doing here? Was she also meeting Chairman? Somehow I doubted it. Wait a minute, had she followed Jasper as well? If she was suspicious of him – and who wouldn't be? – then that made sense. She was a lawyer after all. She could probably tell when her useless boyfriend was keeping secrets. Or maybe she was just there to meet someone else.

Suddenly she emerged from the restaurant, walking very quickly. Her lips were pursed. She was definitely not happy. She hurried out of the hotel, obviously lost in her thoughts. I was now convinced that she had followed Jasper, and was unimpressed to see him with Chairman.

Once she was gone I turned to find out what Vusi was trying to tell me. That's when I realised I had pinned him down with his face squashed against the wall.

"Eish, sorry bra." I released him.

"You could have broken my jaw!" he snapped, touching his face gingerly.

"I'm not that strong. Vusi, I have a plan to find out more about Ayanda." I led him out of the building.

He made a face, testing out his jaw. "I think my tooth is loose."

"We're going to steal her handbag."

"Man, I really think you broke my – Eh?" He turned to stare at me. "Did you say steal?"

"Borrow."

"Did you hit your head?"

I grinned. "It's perfect. We get her bag and we can find out all kinds of things."

"Ja, like what lipstick she likes. Senzo, we're almost criminals already!"

I rolled my eyes. Sometimes I wished Vusi had a little more imagination. "*We're* not going to take it. We're going to get someone else to take it."

"Who would be stupid enough to –" Then Vusi remembered. "Oh."

*

Sipho was one of our best clients. He was what we called a "special case", the kind of customer who could show up five times looking for a solution to the same old problem. He was a middle aged guy built like Dwayne "The Rock" Johnson, but had a high-pitched voice. Not high-pitched like a woman. High-pitched like Alvin and the Chipmunks. He came to me for help and after charging him the usual treatment fee, I explained that the ancestors had given them that voice as a gift, to build character or something. He bought it. Sipho was a die-hard believer in my prophetic powers, and would do almost anything for me. I mean, for Prophet Mazinga.

I sat on the mat in the consulting room in full costume, waiting for him.

"This guy is always late," Vusi grumbled from behind the curtain.

"Sshh! I think I hear somebody."

The door opened and Sipho came in. He looked excited to be there, as usual.

"Hello Prophet," he said, taking a seat opposite me. "I'm happy you called. Did you find out who keeps pissing on my wall?"

I cleared my throat. "The ancestors say there is a man in your hood. There's bad blood between you that goes way back..."

Sipho frowned. "That could be anybody."

"His name is coming to me..." I started to wave my arms like I was having a fit. "Aaahh...Kkkkkk....Sssssss..."

"Sbu!" Sipho shouted. "I should have known."

Bless the guy, he made my job so easy. "It was a difficult task to find this man," I told him solemnly. "The ancestors want you to do something for them in return."

"But I gave you fifty rand last time."

I looked at him. "It's an honour to be asked to serve the spirits in the great beyond, Sipho. If you refuse..."

That was Vusi's cue. Soft wailing came from behind the curtain. "Wooooooooooooooo!"

Sipho jumped. "Gahh!"

"Wooooooo...Sipho..."

"I'll do it!" he shrieked. "Please, please, tell them I will do whatever they want."

The wailing stopped. I nodded. "Wise choice, Sipho. Wise choice. Now, this is what you must do." I took out my phone and showed him Ayanda's photo. "You see this girl?"

"Mmm! Nice."

"Hey, focus. You must go to the offices of Amazi Spring Water, where she works. I'll give you directions. You must get her handbag and bring it here."

Sipho shifted uncomfortably. "Ah, I don't know. What if she calls the police?"

I gave him a look. "We both know you've done this many times. You're a pro. You can do it without getting caught. Don't worry, I'll make sure she gets the bag back. This is a test to see if she is worthy. If *you* are worthy."

Sipho's eyes widened. "I am! I always do everything you ask."

"Yes, you're very loyal. And if you continue to serve them, the ancestors will reward you."

He nodded slowly. "I will make sure you have the bag before the end of the day."

I smiled. That was exactly what I had hoped to hear.

*

A few hours later Sipho sent one of his boys, a kid of about fifteen, with the bag. I knew he would pull it off. Although he was trying to be a law-abiding citizen, Sipho kept backsliding into his old ways. He had thousands of contacts all over the city who could make things happen quickly.

"You should stop bullying Sipho," said Vusi, as I unpacked Ayanda's bag. "He's trying to be a decent guy and you keep getting him in trouble."

"Trust me, he's happy to help," I assured him.

The bag contained the usual things – make-up, a pack of tissues, some mints, an address book, a big folder full of papers and a cellphone. I jumped on the phone, thrilled that we had found something so personal. From what I had seen on her social media I could tell that Ayanda was an open person, so I guessed her phone wouldn't have a password. I was right. I looked through the contact list. There were only a few familiar names – her friends, Jasper and her father.

I decided to read some of her messages, just to get an idea of the kind of person she was. The most recent one was from Jasper, and she hadn't replied. Heh heh! Good.

"Are you reading her messages?" hissed Vusi. "Sies!"

"There's nothing secret here, relax."

I flipped through her photos. Man, this woman took a lot of selfies. Selfies at the office, selfies at the gym, selfies at lunch with her BFFs. In all the pictures she looked happy. There was even one with Jasper at the beach. She looked amazing in her red bikini and Jasper looked like he just won the lottery. My insides twisted with jealousy. I quickly put the phone down and picked up the folder.

"You shouldn't read that," said Vusi nervously. "That's private work stuff."

"I'm not going to sell it on the black market, Vus. Chill. It's boring, anyway."

Vusi leaned forward to get a better look.

"Ah, now you're interested?" I held the folder up so he couldn't see. "It's some kind of contract between Amazi Spring Water and Investor."

"Which investor?"

I shrugged. "It just says investor. I guess they give the same contract to everybody and fill in the names afterwards."

I put the folder back into the bag and picked up the phone again. This time I steered clear of the photos and went back to the messages. One thing I had learned in my years of researching scam victims – I mean clients – was that most people were sentimental. They

30

kept all kinds of things in their bags, cars, drawers and phones, and they never deleted anything until their inboxes got full. Ayanda was the same.

I ignored the messages from people I didn't know and searched for the ones from Jasper. Most of them were short and boring, because Jasper had no imagination. No soul. *I miss u, call me. Hey beautiful. Pick u up at 7.* A lot of them were apologies. *I didnt mean it baby. Pls 4give me. Im sorry Aya.* It was clear that he spent a lot of time screwing things up and trying to make up for it. *Did u get the flowers? Do u like the dress? I got u the Swiss chocolates u <3. Do u like the earrings?*

Ayanda's responses were often brief and impatient. *You can't fix this with earrings. Thank you for the chocolates, goodnight. I said I need time. Please stop, I'll call you when I'm ready.*

I was about to leave the phone again when one conversation caught my interest.
I saw you with Marcus Sithole today.
So? He's a family friend.
You didn't talk about Amazi?
Ja, a bit. He still thinks a partnership would be great. So do I.
My father has made his wishes clear. Please don't go behind his back.
I'm not, we were jst chatting. Relax.

I looked up at Vusi, who was busy studying Ayanda's make-up for some strange reason. "Hey, where have I heard the name Marcus Sithole?"

"He's the telecoms guy," Vusi mumbled, opening a tube of lipstick.

Ah, yes. Now I remembered why Chairman, the man I had seen with Jasper, looked so familiar. He was Marcus Sithole. He really was one of the most successful businessmen in Africa, as he had told Jasper. Although everyone knew him as "the telecoms guy", he had different business interests all over the continent as well as overseas. He was worth millions, and it looked like he was one of many who wanted a slice of Amazi. I had to be right then – ayanda had followed Jasper because she suspected he was meeting with Sithole.

"He's Chairman," I told Vusi excitedly. "He's the guy we saw with Jasper! Apparently they're family friends."

"I'm not surprised," said Vusi. "I told you Jasper's dad hangs out with bigshots these days. Hey, how much do you think this costs?" He held up Ayanda's mascara.

I stared at him in confusion. "How would I know? Why are you looking at make-up anyway? Do you have a secret?"

He quickly put the make-up back into the bag. "Hayi, shut up. Zanele likes mascara. I was thinking maybe if this job works out I can buy her some nice high-class stuff."

Oh God, that was most pathetic thing I had ever heard. The man was so whipped it wasn't funny. I shook my head with a mixture of pity and disgust.

"Hey, don't look at me like that!" he cried. "If you hook up with Ayanda you'll have to start caring about stuff like clothes and lipstick. Women get upset if you don't notice those things."

"You mean *when* I hook up with Ayanda," I corrected him. "Anyway, Chairman and Jasper are definitely more than family friends. You heard them talking at the hotel. They're working together."

"On what?"

"That's the question, Vusi, that's the question."

The two of us packed the bag and zipped it up. I thought back to the conversation I had overheard between Chairman and Jasper. I knew one dirty secret already – Jasper was cheating on Ayanda and had no intention of stopping. But I also wanted to know what he and Chairman were up to. That was no ordinary business meeting, unless ear-pulling was some new corporate tactic. If Jasper was scheming behind Gideon's back and I revealed the truth to Ayanda, I'd be a hero in her eyes. Just to be clear, I was doing this for Ayanda. But the hero thing certainly wouldn't hurt.

Which brought me to the next phase of my plan. I had originally asked Sipho to return the bag, but now I realised that I had a golden opportunity in front of me. I got to my feet and picked up the bag.

"Where are you going?" asked Vusi.

"I need to borrow a nice shirt. That one Zanele got you for her sister's wedding. And the shoes."

His eyes narrowed. "Why?"

"I can't rock up at Amazi in torn jeans and old takkies. Come on, Vus. I'll look after them, I promise."

He sighed and got up. "What are you up to this time?"

"I'm going to be Ayanda's hero."

4.

It's important to plan each step of a scam carefully. I knew that I wanted Ayanda to think of me as the hero who found her stolen bag, but I wasn't ready to meet her in person yet. I still had to work on my disguise. So how was I going to create the idea of a kind, noble guy without actually meeting her? Easy. Word of mouth.

I walked into the Amazi offices the next morning and went straight to the reception desk. Vusi's shirt and shoes were a little big on me, but he had only worn them once and they still looked brand new. I had cut my hair to make sure I came in looking fresh, and I had borrowed a nice leather briefcase. I smiled at the receptionist. She smiled back.

"Good afternoon," I said in my best private school accent. "I'm here to drop this off." I held up Ayanda's bag. "It belongs to Ayanda Zwane. Am I in the right place?"

"Oh!" she gasped. "Someone grabbed it while she was outside the court yesterday! Where did you find it?"

"One of the kids at the shelter where I volunteer had it." I shrugged sadly. "I asked him where he got it but he was too scared to tell me. I assume the police have already been notified?"

"Yes, of course."

I nodded. "I guess there's nothing I can do about that now. I assure you, I gave him a serious talking to and his guardians promised me he would be disciplined." I sighed and shook my head as if the weight of the world was on my shoulders. "He's just a kid – his whole life will be ruined if he's arrested. Nothing is missing. He swore that everything was just the way he found it, and I believe him. But I completely understand that Miss Zwane has to do what she thinks is best. Just tell her I'm so sorry about all of this."

The receptionist melted. "It's not your fault."

"I feel responsible for those kids," I told her. "When they fall back into their old habits, it's such a blow."

"Look, she's free right now. Why don't I call her and you can explain everything to her? I'm sure she'll understand. She loves kids."

Yes, Ayanda did love kids, and I knew that there was no way she would let a poor street kid get arrested. The bag was back, nothing was missing and there was no harm done. She was a big softie. She'd call the cops and tell them to drop the whole thing.

I shook my head again. "I can't wait. I have a plane to catch and I can't afford to miss my meeting in Dubai. But give her my best and tell her I'll be happy to discuss it at the charity event."

"You'll be there?" The woman's eyes lit up. I had her wrapped around my finger.

"Of course; it's the event of the year! I have to go now. Have a lovely day!" I started to walk away.

"Wait, what's your name?" she shouted after me.

I stopped and turned around with a smile. "Senzo. Senzo...Sedibeng." Then I walked out like a boss.

Vusi was waiting for me around the corner. "How did it go?" he asked.

"Perfect. That receptionist is practically in love with me." I laughed. "I can picture what she's going to tell Ayanda. A sophisticated, kind-hearted, handsome stranger walked in and saved the day."

Vusi arched his eyebrows. "Handsome?" I nudged him with my elbow and he cackled. "Seriously, you think this is going to work? Pretending to be rich to impress her?"

"Of course. We just need to convince Jasper to cough up the twenty grand so we can buy tickets and clothes to blend in."

"Why would he do that?"

I grinned. "Because he's stupid."

*

I set up social media accounts so I could follow Ayanda and track the progress of my plan. It worked like a charm. Ayanda put up not one, not two but three posts about the "knight in shining armour" who returned her handbag. #MyHero #NiceGuysFinishFirst #HopeforMankind. Then she posted a query asking if anyone knew Senzo Sedibeng.

"This is dangerous," said Vusi. "What if there's some guy out there with that name and he comes along and she ends up liking him?"

But I refused to get paranoid. Ayanda was already falling for me and she didn't even know it. I read the posts over and over again until my battery died.

Friday night came and Vusi and I went to the restaurant where Jasper, Gideon and Ayanda were scheduled to meet for dinner. They say knowledge is power, but when we sat down at a quiet corner table, I didn't feel powerful. I felt anxious.

"Stop rocking the table!" hissed Vusi. "I'm already stressed by the prices on this menu. We can't order anything! Not even water!"

"Jasper will pay," I assured him, scanning the restaurant. We were seated across the room from the table Jasper had reserved, but he hadn't arrived yet and neither had the Zwanes. "Vus, I haven't seen her in ages."

"You saw her just now on Instagram. And the day before yesterday in the flesh."

"That doesn't count, it was from a distance." I sighed and doodled on the menu with my finger. "What if she's changed? What if I don't recognise her?"

Vusi stared at me as if I'd lost my mind. "How much could she have changed in a few days? Stop rocking the table!"

"I'm not!"

"You're tapping your feet and your knee is knocking the table. You're supposed to be the calm one, remember? We can't both start freaking out!"

I took a deep breath. He was right. I had to keep it together. Ayanda wouldn't see us, so there was no reason to be nervous.

"There's Jasper," said Vusi.

I followed his gaze. Ja, that was Jasper, looking as smug as ever in his three-piece suit. Behind him was Gideon Zwane, and behind him was...Ayanda. My heart jumped. She was even more gorgeous in the flesh. Her hair was tied back and she wore an elegant blue dress. Her figure was curvy perfection. I had seen it before in photos, but I never trusted anything I saw online. Just as I had expected, Ayanda Zwane was still the most beautiful girl I had ever seen.

For a long time I just stared at her. Jasper reached for her hand and when she moved it away I almost cheered. I didn't understand what she was doing with him in the first place. How could a woman like that be fooled by Jasper's swagger? There had to be a rational explanation. Maybe she felt sorry for him.

A waiter approached, blocking my view. I let Vusi order for me while I tried to see past the waiter.

"Stop staring!" said Vusi.

"I can't help it," I sighed. "Look at her!"

But Vusi was right. We were there on a mission and I had to focus. We watched them – or I watched them while Vusi tried to make sense of the menu. Jasper did most of the talking. Ayanda was subdued, attentive toward her father but a little dismissive of Jasper. At one point Gideon left the table and Jasper leaned close to say something to Ayanda. She was quiet at first, but when he reached for her hand again she didn't pull away, and she let him kiss her cheek. My heart sank. She might not have agreed to his proposal, but they were still together.

"Looks like the ancestors have done their work, Prophet Mazinga," said Vusi wryly.

"Shut up," I grumbled. "We both know Jasper's no good. One of these days Ayanda will realise it too."

"With your help," said Vusi.

"With *our* help," I corrected him.

*

I saw a few clients the next morning, but by lunchtime I'd had enough. It was impossible to care about lovers' spats, jealous colleagues and erectile dysfunction when my future with Ayanda hung in the balance.

"We're closing up," I told Vusi.

He emerged from behind the curtain. "Ja, it's time for lunch and I'm starving."

"I mean we're closing for the day. We need to go somewhere."

Vusi groaned. "I don't even want to know."

I grinned at him. "We're going to Amazi."

His eyes boggled.

"Don't worry, we're going in disguise. Prophet Mazinga needs to keep a close eye on his customer Jasper. Can you believe the guy still hasn't sent the money?"

I dragged Vusi along, me in my Prophet Mazinga outfit and him in cracked shades and a beanie. We loitered outside the Amazi offices for a while, waiting to see if anyone interesting turned up, then I decided it was time for decisive action. I strode towards the entrance.

"What are you doing?" hissed Vusi.

"Going in. You wait here."

I walked right up to the reception desk. The receptionist looked at me like I was a stray goat that had wandered in by mistake. If only she knew that the dashing Senzo Sedibeng was hiding under there.

"Can I help you?" she asked.

"I'm looking for Mr Jasper Ndlovu."

Her gaze moved down from my wig to my shoes, like she was scanning me for concealed weapons. "Er, he's not in at the moment. Was he, uh, expecting you?"

"When will he be back?"

"I'm not sure."

"I'll wait."

She looked like she wanted to say something to stop me, but couldn't think of a polite way to let me know she didn't feel comfortable letting a scruffy guy in filthy shoes make himself at home on the suede sofas. So she said, "I...er...o-kay."

I thanked her and took a seat. To my disappointment there was no sign of Ayanda, but five minutes after I sat down Jasper walked in. As he passed the receptionist, she stopped him and whispered a few words. He turned towards me and his eyes widened. For a moment I thought he was going to scream.

He came marching over to me, scowling, the veins in his neck protruding. I remembered this Jasper. This was the Jasper that rearranged my face that day in school after I'd already got a hiding from the teacher. This was the Jasper that liked to break fragile things, like people's noses.

"What the hell do you think you're doing?" he hissed, when he was out of earshot of the receptionist. "Anyone could walk in and see you here!"

"Not even a greeting." I shook my head in disapproval. "Young people of today. No manners. It's no wonder you're so out of touch with the ancestors."

Jasper took a deep breath. "Hello, Prophet Mazinga. What are you doing here?"

"I told you I needed more money. I'm still waiting."

"You'll get it."

"I need it now, or I can't help you."

He glared at me. I glared back.

"You'll get your money as soon as possible," he said.

"If I don't have it by the end of the day, you can say goodbye to your lost lover," I replied solemnly, getting to my feet. "Remember, the spirits can help you...or they can hurt you. Your choice, my friend."

I patted his shoulder and left. Once we were out of sight of the entrance, Vusi hurried to join me.

"So what now, Mr. Lover Boy?"

My phone beeped. I looked down to check the incoming SMS and let out a burst of laughter. Jasper had always been an easy mark. My account balance now stood at a whopping

R20,102. I looked at the number, closed my eyes, opened them and looked again. Twenty thousand rand. In my account. Unbelievable.

I looked at Vusi, smiling so much my cheeks were starting to hurt. "What's your suit size?"

4.

I had never enjoyed shopping. Parting with the little money I had out of necessity wasn't my idea of a fun day out, and I hated standing there debating over a few cents difference in price. But now everything had changed. I had twenty thousand grand to burn and I intended to shop like the other half – with complete abandon.

When we walked into the fancy suit shop, the attendant gave us a look of disdain. Vusi made a beeline for the suit rack and inspected the price tag. His jaw dropped. He turned to me, aghast, and I flashed him a confident smile. This was our turf now and we had as much right to be here as anyone else.

Squaring my shoulders, I walked up to the jewellery counter, picked out a pair of cufflinks and tossed them onto the counter. "I'll take those."

"Are you sure, sir?" The attendant said "sir" in a mocking tone, and for a minute I seriously considered punching him. "They're the most expensive ones we have."

"In that case, give me two," I replied, looking him right in the eyes.

He cleared his throat. "We won't accept credit cards until we run a check on you."

"No problem." I took out my bulging wallet. "I'll pay cash."

Instantly his manner changed. His eyes lit up. "Of course," he gushed. "Will that be all, sir?"

Now that was the tone I'd been waiting to hear – the tone of a man who would bleed himself dry to cater to my every need. Amazing how much a little cold hard cash could change the atmosphere.

"Actually, my friend and I want a few more things," I told him.

He practically jumped over the counter in his hurry to assist me. "Absolutely. What do you need?"

For the next hour we tried on shirt after shirt, suit after suit. We sat with our feet up like kings while Mr Shop Attendant and a colleague brought us shoes and put them on for us. In one day I went from being no one to wearing clothes worth more than a few months' rent.

The effect didn't wear off after we left the suit store. Everywhere we went we were treated with the respect that comes when people think you have money. The world was all about appearances, and I maximized on it. Loaded with shopping bags, we stopped outside a car hire office.

Vusi sighed. "We'd better enjoy the view while we can."

"We'll enjoy it more from inside," I told him, nudging him towards the entrance.

"Senzo, are you crazy?" he hissed. "We shouldn't blow all Jasper's money at once."

"Why not? He has more." I winked at Vusi, then turned to the approaching attendant. "Hi. I'd like that one."

Vusi looked where I was pointing and gasped. It was one of the most expensive cars on display. Maybe blowing the cash wasn't the smartest move, but we were going to a fancy charity event and we had to fit in. Besides, this might be our only chance to experience the high life. After all the years of hustling, we deserved it.

*

Vusi was my boy, but I had never met anyone so whipped in my whole life. The minute we got home from our shopping spree, he called Zanele. Not to say hi or whisper sweet nothings, but to tell her about everything he bought so that she wouldn't be shocked when she saw him in his new threads.

I couldn't believe it. This was supposed to be *our* plan, two guys going on a great adventure, no girls allowed. But ever since Zanele came into the picture it felt like there was an invader in our friendship. She came over that night to see the clothes and give me a lecture about robbing people blind. Even though she had brought us drinks, I was annoyed.

I tried to explain that Jasper was scum and he deserved it, but she wasn't having it.

"It's wrong and you know it," she said.

"If you knew the way Jasper treated me you would understand," I told her.

Vusi nodded. "Ja, it's true. Jasper gave him hell back in the day. He gave everybody hell."

Zanele sighed. "Fine. Maybe Jasper deserves it, but what about Ayanda? Why can't you just be yourself, Senzo? If she's as kind as you think she won't care where you come from."

I laughed. "No way. She's a high-class girl. I have to show her that I'm her equal or she'll never respect me."

"Don't waste your time," Vusi said to Zanele. "Senzo's been dreaming about this girl for years."

"She's my soulmate," I sighed. "My true love."

"Love?" Zanele scoffed. "You don't love her!"

I turned to give her the dirtiest look I could come up with. "What are you talking about? I've been in love with Ayanda since I was a kid!"

"You've *wanted* her since you were a kid," she said, taking a sip of her drink. "You and Jasper are the same. You're fighting over her like she's a toy instead of a person. When you love someone you don't trick them and lie to them."

I snorted. Obviously Zanele had been watching too many romantic movies. "Ja right, like you've never lied to Vusi."

"She hasn't," said Vusi. He sounded so sure.

"And he has never lied to me," said Zanele. They gazed into each other's eyes.

"I would never, babes," said Vusi.

"I know, nunu. You're so sweet."

"You're so beautiful."

"You're so –"

"Ja, ja, ja, enough!" I cried, embarrassed by all their lovey-dovey nonsense.

Zanele snuggled up in Vusi's arms. "You should be honest," she said. "Lies only make things worse."

"Whatever," I replied irritably. "Look, Ayanda's not going to be impressed by some loser from the township. She's not a cleaner in an office, she's a lawyer."

"Uh, he didn't mean that," said Vusi hastily, but it was too late.

Zanele raised her eyebrows. Her nostrils flared. Her lips twitched. Oops. I was in trouble now. "Oh, excuse me, Mr Fancy," she sneered. "I'm not the one who told you to chase women who are too good for you, so don't give me attitude, okay?" She pushed Vusi away and stormed out of the room.

"Why can't you think before you talk?" asked Vusi impatiently, then hurried after her.

I wanted to call him back, but I knew there was no point. I had offended Zanele and Vusi would be mad at me until I apologised. Ag, women! Why did they have to be so difficult? It was Zanele's fault, anyway, telling me I didn't love Ayanda. Of course I loved her. I ignored the little prick of guilt. Fine, maybe lying to her wasn't a good thing, but I was lying because I loved her. That was an excellent reason to lie. In fact it was the best reason in the world.

*

The Galwegian Estates was the sort of place I had only seen on TV. Fancy cars pulled up outside, beautiful people stepped out and cameras flashed furiously as the press tried to capture all the celebrities in their designer outfits.

Vusi whistled, peering through the tinted windows of the car. I had booked our tickets under the name Sedibeng, and they had cost almost as much as the shoes I was wearing. We had found a guy to serve as our chauffeur – there was no way we were driving ourselves, that would just look stupid – and I had planned our entrance down to the second. Paparazzi crowded round the car as we approached, curious to see which famous face would emerge. They were in for a big surprise.

"Remember Vus, attitude," I said as the car rolled to a stop. "This is a normal Saturday night for people like us. Be cool."

"I'm cool," he said, sounding a little offended. "*You're* the problem."

"Don't be stupid, I'm the king of smooth." The driver came to open my door. I took a deep breath, then stepped out.

The flashing lights were more than I had bargained for. I was completely blinded for a minute and I froze, blinking and waiting for my eyes to adjust. I knew I looked good. I was in head-to-toe white like a badass rapper, with diamond-studded crocodile skin shoes on my feet. Ja, it was flashy, but I couldn't resist. I'd probably only get one chance to wear the shoes before some moegoe broke into our flat and jacked them.

Attitude, Senzo, I told myself. You've got this.

I held my head high, looked down my nose at the photographers and walked towards the entrance. Vusi was right behind me, dressed in pink. I'd tried to tell him that pink plus a fake fur collar gave him a kind of big city pimp look, but when he put on the suit he grinned like a kid opening Christmas presents. How could I deprive him of that kind of joy?

We strutted up the steps, the Kingpin and the Pimp, and I heard people whisper as we passed, wondering who we were. Let them wonder. They couldn't see much of our faces behind our new shades. Anyway, after the night was over we'd vanish back into our anonymous lives and no one would give a damn.

Once we were inside, Vusi leaned in and whispered, "What now?"

"Look, there's Jasper, talking to Gideon," I told him. "I'm going over there to see what I can find out. Just relax. If you see Ayanda, buzz me."

But Vusi wasn't listening anymore. He had caught sight of a waiter carrying a tray of champagne glasses. Without another word he started moving towards his target.

"Vusi!"

"Just getting a drink, bra." He called out to the waiter, "Ey, chief!"

"Would you like a glass of champagne, sir?" the waiter asked.

"Just one glass?" Vusi snorted, but reached for a glass anyway. "Where's the bottle?"

I sighed. Knowing how Vusi got when there was free alcohol flowing, I might be stuck handling this job on my own. I looked around for Ayanda but there was no sign of her, so I moved towards Jasper and Gideon. I snatched a glass of champagne from a passing waiter and hid behind a large flower arrangement to eavesdrop.

"Just hear me out," Jasper was saying. "Imagine what a merger between Amazi and Sithole could do for us. We'd expand up into Africa, instead of being on the brink of bankruptcy like we are now. Sithole could be our last chance."

I took a sip of my drink, frowning thoughtfully. Amazi was in that much trouble? No wonder buyers were circling like vultures.

"Forget about it!" said Gideon impatiently, and I got the feeling he and Jasper had discussed this before. "Sithole is a crook. He dresses and speaks like a gentleman but everyone knows the truth." He sighed. "As the head of marketing your job is to push product sales, not buyouts!"

"I get where you're coming from, but –"

"I've spent my entire life building this business from the ground up," Gideon interjected. "Do you know how many families depend on us? Sithole would sell us to the first multinational that came along. People will lose their jobs, Jasper."

I peeked behind the flowers and saw Jasper shrug callously.

"These are tough times. Either we adapt or we die."

Gideon leaned closer to Jasper. "Why are you so keen to entertain his offer?"

Good question. I had my own suspicions based on what I'd overheard between Jasper and Chairman, but Jasper never got a chance to respond. He would probably have lied, anyway. A musical voice interrupted, and at the sound of it my heart leapt.

"Hey, the guests are here. Everyone's asking for you, Pa."

It was Ayanda. I almost knocked the flowers over in my haste to catch a glimpse of her. She came closer, almost floating towards me. I froze, clutching the vase to keep it from falling. She was exquisite, and she was close enough to touch. Almost.

"Sorry, my dear," said Gideon. "We're coming right down."

"By the way, about the Rosenbaums," said Ayanda as they moved away, "remember you said you'd mention the orphanage to them?"

I leaned over, watching them leave.

"I will if I get a chance. My priority right now is finding a capital partner." He looked at Jasper. "The *right* capital partner." He walked on ahead, leaving Ayanda and Jasper to follow.

Jasper sipped his wine and beamed at Ayanda. "I'll introduce you to them, babe."

"That's all right," she replied. "I don't want to go behind Pa's back." Was it just me, or did her tone sound a little cold?

She went on ahead, and Jasper scowled. Nope, it wasn't just me. Good. It took all my willpower to refrain from following her. Well, that and the fact that the vase was ready to topple over and it took me a few minutes to set it right. I decided to go in the opposite direction. It was time to start my play. If I did it well I wouldn't have to chase Ayanda. She would come to me.

The venue had filled up since our arrival and there was no shortage of rich, gullible-looking people to target. As soon as the speeches were over and people began to mingle I set my sights on an elderly white couple. I walked towards them, then stopped to pretend to admire a small bronze warrior statue on display close to where they stood.

"Ah, the proud warrior," I murmured, loud enough for them to hear, and with a touch of sad nostalgia. "Just like the one my father..." I sniffed and turned away from the sculpture to find the white couple watching me. "Oh! Excuse me. I didn't see you there."

"Are you alright?" the woman asked. "You seem to be quite affected by that artwork."

I nodded sadly. "It reminds me of my father. He died a long time ago. In exile."

She drew closer to me, her eyes wide with pity. "Oh, how sad! I'm so sorry. Did you grow up in exile?"

"Yes." I cleared my throat and put on my brave, noble hero face. "It wasn't easy. And when I returned home I had to start from scratch, with nothing."

The elderly lady started to tear up. "You poor, poor child."

I sipped my drink and shook my head. "Don't pity me, please. It made me who I am today."

I spun my tale a while longer, until a few people had gathered to listen and the old woman was so overcome that she pulled me in for a hug. White guilt is a beautiful thing. Useful too, especially at month-end.

I patted the old lady on her back in a dignified fashion, and was just about to lay on a sob story about my long-lost sister when I saw Ayanda coming towards me. She had a curious little smile on her face. I was tempted to push the old woman aside so I could run to Ayanda, sweep her into my arms and carry her away before Jasper turned up. Fortunately I wasn't quite drunk enough for that yet.

I released the old lady, but I only had eyes for Ayanda. She smiled at me. It was the same smile from all those years ago in school, coy and magical.

"Looks like this is where everything's happening," she remarked. "What did I miss?"

The old woman tapped Ayanda's arm. "Ayanda, dear. You absolutely have to meet this lovely young man. Senzo, I believe?" She turned to me to confirm.

Ayanda extended her hand and suddenly I couldn't remember my name.

"I, uh, yes, uh..."

"I'm Ayanda Zwane." When our hands touched, I felt a shiver of pleasure.

I cleared my throat and pulled myself together. "Senzo. Senzo Sedibeng."

Her eyes widened. "You!" For a moment I thought she was onto me already, then I remembered the business with her handbag. "You're the one who brought back my bag!"

I smiled. "Yes, that was me."

"I've been trying to find you but you're not on social media," she gushed.

I nodded, trying to look cool. "I'm not really into that stuff. I'd like to start, but I never seem to find the time. Thank you for not sending the police after my young friend. I really think he can turn his life around."

"Oh, it was the least I could do," she said. "When I heard the whole story I felt so bad for the poor kid. He should have just asked me for help. I would have given him some money."

"You'll be surprised how proud orphans can be."

"I'm so happy to finally meet you!" she said with a little laugh. I felt a very pleasant tingle moving through my body. Yep, this was love for sure. "The receptionist at the office won't stop talking about you, you know," she went on. "I think she's started a fan club."

I laughed. "I only did what any decent person would."

"Unfortunately there aren't enough decent people anymore."

She was still holding my hand, and I wasn't going to complain. She beamed. I beamed back, and then I saw Jasper standing behind her and leering suspiciously at me.

"Have we met?" he asked.

To my disappointment, Ayanda let go of my hand.

"Definitely not," I replied, adjusting my shades. "I think I'd remember that face."

Jasper frowned. "Are you sure?"

I pretended to pause to think about it. "Unless you were at that clothing drive for the homeless last month. Are you into charity work?"

"He isn't," said Ayanda hastily. "But I am."

"Oh, really? I do a lot of charity work in KZN," I said, "organizing volunteers to build schools and orphanages that side. I guess it's something I picked up from my years in exile. The struggle isn't over yet, you know."

"Is that right?" Jasper sneered.

I nodded solemnly. "Ja. The country needs more than B.E.E. That's why I wanted to come back, make some money and use it to make a difference in people's lives."

Ayanda sipped from her glass. "It's interesting that I never heard of you before you returned my purse."

I let out a chuckle. "Yes, I prefer to do it anonymously. It's not for the publicity, you know. It's for the people. Especially the kids."

She nodded in excitement. "I know exactly what you mean!"

Out of the corner of my eye I saw Jasper roll his eyes in disgust. To his left was Vusi, approaching with two glasses. I waited until Vusi was right next to us, then I shifted slightly, knocking into him and making him spill wine all over Jasper.

Vusi gasped.

Jasper was livid. "What the hell? Look what you've done!"

A wet patch had spread down the front of his pants. It looked as though he had peed himself. It was the best thing I had seen all week.

"I'm so sorry," I gushed. "I didn't see you there, Vusi." I winced at the stain. "That looks bad, my brother."

Jasper glared at me.

"You probably want to rinse that off before it dries," Ayanda suggested.

Jasper clicked his tongue furiously. "Damnit!" He stormed away in a huff.

When I looked back at Ayanda, I saw her smile.

"I'm sorry," I said.

"It was an accident," she replied.

Vusi downed his wine and looked forlornly at the other glass, the contents of which had been soaked up by Jasper's crotch. "Let me get you a refill."

"You don't have to –" I began, but he was already gone.

As soon as I realised that Ayanda and I were finally alone, my confidence vanished and I was that teenager standing in front of the class again, trying desperately to impress her. She glanced at me. I glanced at her. Okay, maybe I did more than glance. Maybe I stared like a love struck schoolkid. Ayanda looked away shyly and cleared her throat. I fidgeted with my tie. I wanted to say something clever to fill the awkward silence, but my brain had gone fuzzy.

"So how long have you been back in South Africa?" she asked, coming to my rescue.

"Oh, not long," I said, relieved to be back on track. "I work a lot, so I don't have much of a social life. I have very few friends here. I'm still settling in, discovering new places. Trying new things." I smiled. "It would be nice to have a guide to show me around the city of lights."

"Hey, I'd me more than happy to."

"Really?" I pretended to be surprised by the offer. "I don't want to be a bother."

"No bother at all," she assured me, sipping her drink. "Just let me know when."

I was about to respond when her buddy Mandla turned up.

"Hey chomie," said Ayanda warmly.

"I think your friend there has had a bit too much to drink, hey," he said, pointing.

We turned just in time to see Vusi lifting silverware off the tables and stuffing it into his pockets. Ayanda gasped. I groaned.

"This is so disappointing," I said, shaking my head. "And he was doing so well."

"What do you mean?" she asked.

"Well, he's actually a former hobo," I declared. Vusi would have to forgive me. I was sure he'd get over it; he had forgiven much worse. "I took him off the streets, cleaned him up and bought him a suit. I'm trying to rehabilitate him back into normal society."

"Ja, neh," said Mandla, eyeing Vusi with disdain. "You can take a man out the gutter, but you can't take the-"

"Stop it, Mandla," said Ayanda sharply. "The poor guy. Senzo, it's not a problem. The work you're doing is very important. I really wish there were more men like you. It's just silverware, after all. It can be replaced."

"Thank you," I said. "That means a lot to me."

I watched Vusi stumble over to the DJ and whisper in his ears. Suddenly the music switched to a throbbing house beat. Vusi launched into a dance, right there in the middle of all the guests. An elderly white woman, grinning from ear to ear, got up to join him. Within seconds the floor was packed with elderly people getting their groove on. I looked at Ayanda, worried that my homeboy had ruined her party, but she was smiling.

I did the only sensible thing a man in my position could do. With a casual shrug, I leapt onto the dance floor and started doing the pantsula, much to the excitement of the old white people. Soon they were all trying to imitate me. It was classic. I spotted Jasper return from the bathroom, and I knew I had to seize my chance. I hurried over to Ayanda, took her hand and led her to the dancefloor. She didn't resist. I started dancing around her and soon she let loose and busted a couple of moves of her own.

Across from us, Vusi was in the middle of a dance battle with an elderly white man, who made up for his lack of agility with sheer exuberance and determination. The crowd cheered, clearly favouring the old white guy. I turned back to Ayanda, but not for long. Mandla interrupted again, tapping my shoulder.

"You need to stop that friend of yours before he burns this place down!" he hissed.

Vusi was dancing around topless, waving a flaming shirt over his head. The old white man was in the process of unbuttoning his own shirt and the people gathered around them, who were equally hammered, were going nuts. In a matter of minutes the party had spun completely out of control, and it was fantastic...

...Until Gideon came running towards us with a fire extinguisher. He blasted away at the burning shirt, eliciting moans of disappointment from the onlookers.

"Okay," he gasped, "party's over."

The elderly white man patted Gideon on the back, laughing hard. "I haven't had this much fun in a long time, Gideon. Not since the sixties at least."

Gideon put down the extinguisher. "Apologies about this, Mr. Rosenbaum, but it was a fire hazard."

Mr Rosenbaum waved away the apology. "I'm not wearing a shirt. Call me Stuart, please."

"Okay, er, Stuart." Gideon nodded towards Vusi. "I don't know how he got past security, but I assure you he wasn't on the invite list." He scowled at Vusi. "I want you out of here immediately."

"Oh, don't be so hard on the young man," said Mrs Rosenbaum. "We haven't had this much fun in years."

Mr Rosenbaum grabbed his wife's ass and they giggled like kids.

Gideon's eyes widened. "I'm glad you enjoyed yourselves."

"Listen, let's meet next week," Mr Rosenbaum suggested. "We can finalize that deal we've been discussing."

Gideon's face lit up. "That would be wonderful, Stuart. Thank you."

"No, thank *you*," said Mrs Rosenbaum, and she and her husband walked off, humming as they went.

Gideon turned to face me and Vusi. His smile had vanished. I racked my brain to find something charming to say before he kicked us out in disgrace.

"I don't know who the hell you two are but..." He laughed and shook his head in disbelief. "I guess I should thank you."

I was too stunned to respond. He left us, and soon the guests had all streamed out of the venue and the only people remaining were me, Vusi, Ayanda and Jasper. A waiter appeared, set down his tray on a nearby table and started collecting the used glasses.

"Thanks for a great evening, Ayanda," I said. I didn't want to leave, but I couldn't think of an excuse to linger. I gave her a wistful smile, took Vusi by the arm and started towards the door.

"Wait!"

I turned back to face her, my heart pounding with hope. "Yes?"

"Would you be interested in helping out at the orphanage with me? We're always in need of more hands, and since you're involved in so much charity work, I thought..."

"I'd be honoured," I said. "Anything for the kids."

"Let's toast to that," she suggested suddenly, snatching two still-full glasses from the waiter's tray. She handed one to me.

Jasper glowered at me as I reached out to clink glasses with his girlfriend. He cleared his throat loudly. "Shouldn't you be leaving now? It's getting late."

I took a few swigs from the glass, then put it back on the tray. "Yes, it is."

Ayanda took a card out of her purse and held it out. "Give me a call tomorrow and we'll work out the details."

I took the card. "Thanks. I will." I allowed myself one last look at her beautiful face, then grabbed Vusi and made my exit. "I think that went well," I told him as we walked towards the car.

"The floor is moving," he replied. "I think it's telling us to dance."

I patted his shoulder. It had been an incredible night, the best night of my life, and I was convinced it was only going to get better. As it turns out, I was wrong.

5.

I woke up Monday morning to find Vusi standing over me, waving a newspaper in my face. I sat up and rubbed my eyes.

"Look what you've got us into," he said frantically. "Shit! Zanele's going to kill me!"

"What are you talking about?" I took the paper. It was open to the society pages, and there was a full spread on Saturday night's charity event. There was even a photo of me and Vusi emerging from the venue. Vusi was topless and I was grinning like a fool. I nodded my approval. "We look good."

"Good?" Vusi snatched the paper. "Good? How am I supposed to explain this to Zanele? I promised her I'd keep a low profile! I was supposed to be working, not partying!"

"You *were* working," I reminded him.

"This is your fault!" He crumpled up the paper and tossed it aside.

"Ja, tell her that. She's going to blame me, anyway."

"Yoh, what if my grandmother sees it?" Vusi gasped. He sank onto my mattress, distraught.

I shook my head. "Chill, bra. You're famous! Sort of."

"This is serious, Senzo. Zanele's already upset that we're still doing the Prophet Mazinga scam. I promised I would stay out of trouble, man! I *promised*!"

I sighed. I wanted to be a good friend and listen to Vusi's woes, but I was sick of Zanele's whining. She had never liked me and the feeling was mutual. Besides, I had made plans to meet Ayanda that morning and I didn't want anything getting in the way.

I gave Vusi a pat on the back. "Stop worrying about it. Look, I'm going to meet Ayanda today so you have the whole morning to yourself. Go spend some time with Zanele. We still have some money left. Take her out for Nandos or something."

He gave me a look. "She'll know something's up, she's not stupid."

I kept my opinion on that to myself. "Confidence is key, my man. Remember that."

He snorted. "When will you be back?"

I shrugged. "Who knows? Maybe never." I winked at him and went to take a shower.

*

Ayanda had invited me to her office to discuss her favourite subject – charity. We sat down in one of the smaller conference rooms and a secretary brought us coffee and biscuits. It wasn't exactly my idea of the perfect date – people kept walking past the glass doors so there was zero privacy – but we were alone and I had her full attention. I decided to use the opportunity to find out more about *my* favourite subject – Ayanda.

"So you're a lawyer," I said, smiling over my coffee cup. "I'm impressed."

She laughed. "Actually, it's not that exciting. I'm part of Amazi's legal team, so mostly I deal with contract law. The really interesting work is what I do for the legal clinic in the township."

"Oh, you volunteer there as well?" I asked, like I hadn't read her CV word for word twelve times.

She nodded. "It's so rewarding."

"What sort of cases do you handle? Domestic disputes?"

"Sometimes, though that's not my area. Mostly I work on labour-related cases, situations where people haven't been paid what they were promised and so on. A lot of people enter into verbal agreements, and then when they're cheated they don't know what to do, so they come to us for advice. It's important for people to know their rights."

Ag shame, she looked so cute when she was passionate about something. I nodded in understanding. "Yes, absolutely."

"For instance, last week I spoke to someone who was the victim of a scam."

I choked on my coffee. "Really?" I reached for a tissue from the box in the middle of the table. "That's...interesting."

"You won't believe how many con artists are running around out there, deceiving innocent people," she went on. She didn't look cute anymore. She looked angry. "It's unacceptable. I mean these people call themselves doctors and pastors and prophets, and claim to be able to heal all kinds of diseases which they know nothing about. They're just swindlers, plain and simple. Frauds."

I cleared my throat. "Terrible, indeed. And, eh, how do you help the clients – I mean the victims?"

"I start by telling them the obvious – don't give money to someone until they've treated you or given you medicine." She sighed. "Some people are very naive, you know. They'll pay a deposit and then the medicine never comes."

"Mmm. I see." My heart was pounding, but I had to know more. Was she talking about con artists in general or Prophet Mazinga specifically? "I can see how it would be easy to prove that someone wasn't a real doctor, but what about a prophet? How can you be sure that he doesn't have the gift?"

Ayanda rolled her eyes. "I don't believe in 'the gift' at all," she said, making quotation marks with her fingers, "but a lot of people do and there's nothing I can say to change their minds. But if someone has a history of empty promises, it's safe to say that person's a charlatan."

Charlatan. I swallowed. That word had been hurled at me before, but I didn't want to think about it. I cleared my throat again. "Yes. Hmm. So...what other volunteer work do you do?"

Ayanda paused to finish her biscuit. "Well, I help out at an old age home."

"Tell me about that," I said eagerly. I wasn't really interested in hearing about old timers, but I didn't want her to revisit the dangerous topic of charlatans. Besides, according to Zanele women like a man who listens.

Before she could continue, someone opened the door and walked in without knocking. I looked up to see my old enemy, Jasper.

"You again," he sneered.

"Hi," I replied with a big smile.

"Jasper, haven't you ever heard of knocking?" Ayanda asked impatiently. "You can see we're in a meeting."

Jasper stared at us in surprise. "I didn't know the company was hiring former exiles."

"Don't be ridiculous." Ayanda sighed and gave him an unimpressed look. "Senzo's going to come do some work at the orphanage. So if you don't mind..."

It took a second for Jasper to take the hint. "Oh. Er, okay. Ja, sure. I just wanted to make sure we're still on for tonight."

"*Still* on? I thought I said I had to work."

I smirked at Jasper. That's right fool, I told him with my eyes. Ayanda would rather work than hang out with you.

"Baby, come on –" he pleaded.

"Jasper." It was clear from the frown on Ayanda's face that she was getting fed up. "Please."

"We'll talk about this later," he decided, finally stepping out. He gave me a long, threatening stare before closing the door and walking away.

"Sorry about that," said Ayanda.

"Don't apologise. If he's bothering you at work I'm sure there are steps you can take." I arched my eyebrows. "Legal steps."

She smiled. "No, it's not like that. Jasper and I have been seeing each other for a long time, actually."

Seeing each other. Hmm. No wonder she was confused. As far as I was concerned either you were dating or you were having a fling. What the hell was *seeing each other* supposed to mean?

I leaned back in my chair. "It seemed like he was bothering you."

She rolled her eyes. "He can be so selfish and demanding sometimes. But other times...well, it's complicated."

It wasn't complicated at all. It was simple. All she had to do was dump Jasper and date me. But I said, "Sure," and gave her an understanding nod, because Senzo Sedibeng was that kind of guy.

"Now, back to the orphanage." Ayanda finished off her coffee and looked at me.

"I can start whenever you like," I told her. "Like I said, I'm always looking for opportunities to make a difference."

"It's wonderful that you're so enthusiastic about it," she said, smiling. "A lot of people just do charity work to keep up appearances."

"Well, I can't speak for those people."

"No, of course not. You're a true hero." She reached out to put her hand over mine, and I swear the world stopped for a second. "I'll never forget that you came all the way over here to return my bag."

"It was my pleasure," I said. "I'm just glad it all worked out."

She nodded, then cleared her throat and moved her hand. "Uh, yes. Well, I'll be at the St. Martins orphanage all day this Saturday, so that would be a good time for you to stop by. I can show you the ropes and introduce you to the nuns and the kids."

St Martins. How long had it been since the last time I set foot in that place? Years, and the plan had been to keep it that way. But how could I refuse Ayanda? I put on my most charming smile.

"Saturday is perfect."

*

"You're an idiot," said Vusi, later that day.

After a slow afternoon we had retired to our usual table at the shebeen. We were sipping beers that we had bought on credit, as usual, even though we still had a little bit of Jasper's money left.

"You, working with kids?" Vusi shook his head. "You hate kids, remember?"

"Minor detail," I replied.

"You swore you'd never go back to an orphanage. Especially *that* orphanage."

I shrugged. "I have no choice. That's where Ayanda volunteers."

"It's a terrible idea."

"It'll be fine. A man can change, you know." I took a big gulp of beer. "Maybe I'll decide that I love orphanages. Little kids laughing, playing, having fun... maybe I'll love those little bastards. Besides, I have info on Jasper now. It's only a matter of time before Ayanda dumps him."

"Really? What info do you have?"

"Look at the facts," I said confidently. "We know Jasper is a two-timing loser. We know he's working with Chairman to get Gideon to sell the company. If they succeed, Jasper will get a cut."

"But Gideon's not going to sell," said Vusi.

"He doesn't want to, but they must have a plan." I rubbed my chin thoughtfully. "A guy like Chairman doesn't become a bigshot by luck." And then it came to me. "Ayanda!"

Vusi groaned. "Can't you spend five minutes without saying her name?"

"No, I mean she's the answer!" I snapped my fingers, proud of myself for figuring it out. "That's why he's so desperate to marry her. Once he's part of the family, he'll have more control over the company! He might even convince Ayanda and Gideon to give him more shares, and then he and Chairman can take over Amazi!"

Vusi frowned. "That's a big accusation, man. You'll need proof."

"I'll get proof," I assured him.

He looked unconvinced.

"Come on, everything's finally going our way!" I reminded him. "Whatever comes, we'll handle it. Team?" I extended my hand for a high five, but he left me hanging. I dropped my hand. "Fine. Stay here and sulk. I'm going to get another round."

I left him and moved towards the front. The place was packed as usual and the waiters were all busy. I spotted Big Mama at the counter, directing a new cashier who seemed to be struggling.

"You're here again?" she said when she saw me. "Didn't I tell you to stop drinking so much?"

"Ah, Big Mama, don't be like that." I leaned over the counter and grinned at her. "I'm your best customer!"

"Be careful of this one," she said to the cashier. "He likes to buy on credit."

The girl giggled.

"I paid last month!"

"Hmm," said Big Mama, but her eyes twinkled and I could tell she wasn't really angry. "What now? Second round? Third?"

"Second," I laughed.

She gave the girl my order and helped her ring it up, then paused to chat with me.

"You're in a good mood," she said, and then frowned. "I hope you're not up to something. You and that Vusi, always causing trouble."

"Why do you always think I'm up to something?" I protested, feeling a little bit hurt.

"Because you're always up to something." She poked my arm. "Tell me. What now? Another scam? Selling holy water?"

I snorted. We had graduated from that a long time ago. "Nah, nothing like that." I thought of Ayanda and couldn't help smiling.

Big Mama whistled. "Is it a girl? My God! Are you finally getting serious about life?"

My reply was a mysterious shrug.

"Hmm!" Big Mama beamed and folded her thick arms on top of the counter. "I like this. Who is she? A nice girl, neh? Not like that other one."

"She's a very nice girl," I told her proudly. "A lawyer."

"Eh? How did you find a lawyer?"

"Ah, Big Mama!"

She laughed. She had a big, loud, booming laugh, and when she laughed her whole body shook. It was like she was laughing from deep inside. It always made me smile. I started telling her about Ayanda. To be honest I was always looking for an excuse to talk about her and Vusi was getting sick of it, so it was nice to have someone who actually wanted to know.

"And she volunteers at St Martins Orphanage, and she asked me to come and help out, so I'm going there tomorrow and we'll spend the whole day together." I sighed happily.

"You're going back to St Martins?"

I nodded.

"You said you were never going back."

Why was everyone so hung up on what I had said? Wasn't I allowed to change my mind? I looked at Big Mama and realised that her smile had vanished. She looked worried. Ag shame, she was probably afraid that it would be traumatic for me to go back.

"Don't worry," I said. "I'll be fine. I won't know any of the kids there, and there are probably new nuns. It will be like a different place."

"Ja, maybe," she mumbled. "Eh, I have to go take care of something. Later, neh?"

She hurried away through the crowded shebeen before I even had a chance to say bye. I watched her leave, then shrugged, picked up the beers and carried them back to the table.

*

I couldn't wait until Saturday to speak to Ayanda, so I called her the next morning, just to hear her voice. Of course I had to pretend I was calling for a reason, and our new common ground seemed like the perfect excuse.

"I was just calling to find out if you've heard about the seminar at Wits," I said when she answered. I was sitting in the consulting room with a newspaper open in my lap. There was an advert on the left page. Some international bigshot was going to talk about community building through the arts. It seemed like the sort of thing Ayanda would be into.

"Oh, yes! It sounds wonderful. Unfortunately I can't make it. Are you going?"

"I don't know." I turned the page, no longer interested in the seminar. "I have meetings that day, but I'll try to stop by. How are things going at the office?"

"Not bad," she replied. "We have a meeting with some investors in a few minutes. I'm sure you remember the Rosenbaums from the party?"

I laughed. "How could I forget?"

"Well, you made an impression that worked in Amazi's favour. Thanks, by the way."

"My pleasure. So that's what your typical day is like, huh? Meetings with investors?"

"Yes, a lot of meetings, a lot of phone calls, a lot of reading long, complicated contracts, and a lot of filing. But this afternoon I'm going to stop by the legal clinic. I told you I help out there, didn't I?"

"Yes, you mentioned it." There was no way I would forget that the love of my life worked with people who might be Prophet Mazinga's clients. "You work there on weekdays, too?"

"Only when I have a couple of hours free. I'm really concerned about the con artists operating in the township," she said, and my heart almost stopped. "So far people don't want to tell me much – I guess they're scared the conmen will come after them."

"What do you mean?" I asked.

If people were too scared to talk, then maybe I didn't have to worry after all. Ayanda didn't understand kasi politics. She was from the world of contracts and ethics. I came from the world of rough justice. I had never actually hurt anyone for badmouthing Prophet Mazinga, but I had certainly made my share of convincing threats.

"Well, they're upset that the medicine doesn't work but they still believe in those things, you know?" Ayanda clicked her tongue, exasperated. "They don't want to anger the ancestors by turning on a prophet. I don't even know which prophet is supposed to be the false one. There are so many! Prophet Chulumba, Dr Albert, Pastor Josiah, Prophet Mazinga. It's a mess. Even the clients can't keep them all straight."

My heart pounded when she mentioned Prophet Mazinga. "Yes, I can imagine. What are you going to do?"

"There's not much I can do if the people who complained don't come back," she said. "That's one of the problems we face. People come for legal advice, but when they find out how the law works or what's at stake they change their minds. They don't want to go through the whole process if nothing will come of it, or if they might put themselves at risk."

I murmured in agreement.

"Have you heard of any of these prophets?"

I licked my lips, thinking fast. "Uh, sure."

"Do you think they're honest?"

I chose my words carefully. "I think they're just trying to survive. When times get hard and they need to pay the bills, maybe they stretch the truth a little. I'm sure they don't even think about the legal side of it."

"Hmm. You have a point," she agreed softly. "Maybe I should organise a workshop at the legal clinic and invite them."

I wanted to laugh. I could picture all the prophets and pastorpreneurs sitting in a room, listening to Ayanda lecture them and then agreeing to change their ways. Ja, right.

"The Rosenbaums have arrived," said Ayanda. "I have to go. It was nice talking to you, Senzo."

"You, too. Enjoy the rest of your day."

I hung up, realising exactly how much was at stake where Ayanda was concerned. It was bad enough that she thought I was a rich self-made former exile. If she found out I was also Prophet Mazinga, it would all be over.

The door opened and Vusi walked in clutching a plastic bag filled with fresh chips.

"And then? What's wrong with you?" He reached into the bag and handed me one packet of chips.

"I was talking to Ayanda."

"Eish, not Ayanda again!" Vusi shook his head. "A client is coming in ten minutes, man. You must focus."

He was right. I couldn't let Ayanda's upper class sentiments distract me. It was easy for her to talk when she was born into money. People like me had to hustle. That was just the way it was. I popped one hot chip into my mouth, then pulled the dreadlock wig over my head. Time for work.

*

The next day me and Vusi got a surprise visitor. Jasper turned up without warning, storming in moments after another client had left. Vusi was just about to come out from behind the curtain when Jasper entered. Vusi quickly pulled the curtain shut. Fortunately Jasper was too upset to notice the curtain moving.

"What the hell are you doing?" he demanded, glaring at me.

I looked up at him. "Ah, Mr Ndlovu. Have a seat."

"Don't tell me to have a seat!" he barked. "You said you would fix things with my woman, but ever since I came to you things have only gotten worse!"

"Worse? Worse how?"

"She's met someone. Some brat who came back from exile."

I had to bite my lip to keep from laughing. "Surely this man is not a threat to you."

"Of course not! But he shares her silly little interests. Charity and volunteering, that kind of nonsense. Ayanda loves that stuff."

"Hmm." I scratched my chin thoughtfully. "Yes, I see. I see. It is a test, my friend."

Jasper scowled. "A test?"

"Yes. The ancestors want to know whether you are truly worthy, so they have sent you some competition. This is a good thing!"

He looked sceptical. "How is it a good thing that some idiot is moving in on my territory?"

I smiled. "If – I mean when – you win her back from this man, she will never leave you again. I told you this was a complicated case. It's going to take time. You must be patient."

"You'd better be right, prophet," he said menacingly. "I paid you a lot of money."

"Trust me, Mr Ndlovu, your money is hard at work."

He seemed satisfied, at least for now. Without another word he turned around and left. The curtain twitched and Vusi peeped out.

"We're dead," he whispered.

"Relax, Vus. Everything's fine. He believed me."

"Are you sure?"

I grinned at him. "Of course."

*

On Saturday morning I stood in front of St Martins, feeling a little nervous. Okay, *very* nervous. There was a new sign, freshly painted, and the old gate had been replaced by a bigger one with a lock. There was a higher fence, too. Times had changed and even a Catholic orphanage wasn't safe from crooks. I realised I hadn't been on that street for a long, long time.

The thing is, I didn't graduate from the orphanage like the other kids. I didn't go through the ceremony and special dinner the orphanage always organised for the kids who passed matric. By Grade Eleven I was already sure that the education system was never going to work for me, but there was no way Vusi's gogo would let him quit school and I couldn't abandon him. So I stayed. I made it through matric and my grades weren't bad. But I couldn't stick with the orphanage.

When I turned sixteen I figured I was old enough to look after myself. I was tired of being told what to do, what to think, how much God loved me. Ja, right. If He loved me why was my life so freaking hard? I took the things I had accumulated over the years and ran away. The nuns weren't really in a position to bring me back. Sometimes kids left to make their own way in the world, and the nuns had to focus on looking after the ones who remained. Vusi begged me to come stay with him but I knew his granny had enough mouths to feed already. Sometimes I spent a few nights with him, but most of the time I moved from one place to another, staying with friends.

It was around that time that I met Big Mama. She had a spaza shop on the corner near the school, and she let me sleep there in exchange for guarding her stock. By the time I finished school she had three more spaza shops, and we celebrated Vusi's 21st in her brand new shebeen.

In the early days I would pass by the orphanage sometimes, just to see if it was still standing. After some time I stopped. I didn't want to be reminded of the past. I wanted to move on. I started avoiding the area altogether.

Now, over a decade later, there I was, standing at the gate like a stranger. The padlock wasn't locked, so I reached out and opened the gate. Then I took a deep breath and stepped inside. The grounds looked nice and well-kept. There were some flowers near the front door and I wondered whether Sister Lucy was still there to water them every day.

The front door opened and Ayanda came out, looking gorgeous as always.

"Hi!" she said, smiling. "I'm glad you made it. Come in."

She led me down the familiar corridors. It was like I had gone back in time. I remembered all the times I got into trouble for running through those corridors. I could almost hear Sister Lucy's voice: "Hey wena, no running in here! How many times do I have to tell you?"

I followed Ayanda to one of the offices, and when we stopped at the door my heart started racing. This used to be Sister Lucy's office.

"The nuns have to meet you before they let you work with the kids," Ayanda explained, knocking on the door. "There are forms to fill as well, but don't worry. The nuns are always happy to have volunteers."

A voice told us to come in and Ayanda opened the door and stepped inside. I followed her nervously, keeping my head lowered just in case, but it wasn't Sister Lucy. I recognised the lady as one of the younger nuns who had been there during my time. She had been in charge of another group, and I don't think she even knew my name. She shook my hand with no sign of recognition.

After I filled out their forms – using my fake name, of course – Ayanda introduced me to two more nuns. I didn't recognise either of them, and Sister Lucy was nowhere to be found. Once I let Ayanda show me around, my confidence came back. I slipped into the role of Senzo Sedibeng, child of exile, with ease, and I could tell Ayanda was impressed. I was compassionate, kind, brave and noble. I was finally living up to my own hype.

Okay, so maybe I was a little uncomfortable when she introduced me to the kids, but Ayanda didn't seem to notice. The person who did notice was Mandla, who showed up about half an hour after I arrived. Apparently he didn't have a job or a life of his own. Why was he always hanging around like an overprotective big brother? He kept giving me shady looks, like he knew I wasn't who I said I was. Not that there was any way he could be onto me. I had been in the con game for years. Nosy guys in silk cravats were no match for me. What kind of person wore a cravat in real life anyway?

Just when I thought I'd be able to fake my way through the day, Ayanda did the unthinkable. She left me alone with the little monsters, and it was all downhill from there. Somehow I found myself on my hands and knees in one of the classrooms, surrounded by kids. One of them had drawn a flower on my forehead, my new shirt was creased, there was a little boy on my back and an army of brats tugged at my clothes, pulling me in all directions. It was like being attacked by wolves, except worse.

I didn't like kids. They were loud and messy and never minded their own business. They had no boundaries, asked stupid questions, and their hands always seemed to be covered in something sticky. Where was the appeal? I thought I could do it for Ayanda, but I was wrong. Within a few minutes I'd had enough.

I stood up without warning and the little boy slid right off my back and toppled over. It was funny until he started to cry.

"Don't even think about it," I warned him, and he stopped immediately. "Okay, everybody. Play time's over. It's nap time now."

"We don't want to sleep," one of the brats declared. Her name was Nomfundo, and she was the most vocal member of the group. In my opinion she had far too much attitude for a seven-year-old.

I shook my head. "Good girls and boys take a nap when grownups –"

"Tell us a story first!" she demanded, to yells of affirmation from her posse.

"Nope! It's nap time. Go to sleep."

The yells got even louder. I covered my ears to drown out the noise and the little monsters started tugging at my clothes. It was too much for anyone to take.

"Okay, okay!" I cried. "You win." I sighed in exasperation and sat cross-legged on the floor.

The kids settled down around me, looking at me in excitement.

"Okay. Let's do this." I thought for a second, and a brilliant plan began to form in my mind, as usual. I cleared my throat and began my story. "Once upon a time a long, long time ago, there was an orphanage just like this one, filled with little boys and little girls, just like all of you."

"Oohs" and "Aahs" went up from the kids.

"They also refused to take a nap when the nice man asked them." I dropped my voice to a stage whisper. "But what they didn't know was that each time they refused, Themba was watching from inside the cupboard." I pointed at a nearby cupboard. "A cupboard just like that one."

The kids were on tenterhooks, eyes wide as saucepans.

"Themba would write down all the names of the little boys and girls who refused to take a nap," I went on.

"Who is Themba?" asked Nomfundo.

I put on my spookiest voice. "Themba - was - a - TOKOLOSHI!"

The kids gasped in terror.

I grinned, proud of myself. "When all the children at the orphanage finally went to sleep at night, Themba the tokoloshi would climb out of the cupboard and look for all the children who were refusing to take a nap..."

Nomfundo swallowed hard. "W-what would he do t-to them?"

"He would bite their little toes off. One by one. Mmmm, so tasty!"

Some of the kids began to cry. Heh heh, served them right for misbehaving.

"Ag, shame," I said in mock sympathy. "What's wrong now?"

Their wailing only intensified.

"We don't like that story," Nomfundo moaned.

"If you go and take a nap right now, Themba won't write you down on his list," I told them solemnly. "I promise."

The kids scrambled to get their sleeping mats and pillows, and in a few minutes they were all lying still. Mission accomplished. I was about to take a seat and relax when I heard voices in the corridor. I moved towards the door, afraid that one of the nuns had figured out who I was and was coming to ruin everything. But it wasn't the nuns, it was Mandla and Ayanda.

"But he's awful with the kids, Aya," Mandla was saying. "You can tell he doesn't have a clue what he is doing."

I scowled. I would have to do something about that guy before he screwed up my plans.

"Why are you so threatened by Senzo?" asked Ayanda.

I nodded. Good question.

"Threatened!" Mandla sounded horrified. "He mixes blue and brown. I mean, who does such a thing? It's a crime against humanity."

I looked down at the clothes I'd bought with Jasper's hard-earned cash. What was he talking about? I looked fantastic.

Ayanda sighed. They were right by the door now. "If you want to see how bad he is we can stop and check."

I jumped away from the door and threw myself into the chair behind the teacher's desk a moment before the door opened. Ayanda and Mandla poked their heads into the classroom. All the kids were napping. I gave Mandla a smug smile and pressed a finger to my lips. Ayanda gave me a thumbs up sign, and Mandla stared open-mouthed at the sleeping children. Slowly Ayanda closed the door, and I breathed a sigh of relief.

How much longer did I have to hang around this place? I looked up at the clock on the wall and was horrified to see that I had only been there two hours. Two hours! Right then I knew it was going to be a long, long day. It had better be worth it in the end. I imagined Ayanda and I driving off into the sunset in a shiny Maserati, and grinned.

*

The day dragged on. I had gone into it expecting to spend all day with Ayanda, but I had only seen her for a few minutes. The kids were a lousy consolation prize, and by the time we got around to arts and crafts I was impatient and irritable.

I sat with my legs propped up on the table, studying a series of meaningless squiggles on a page. I looked at the culprit responsible for the squiggles, a kid of about five or six.

"This is terrible," I told him. "You call this art?"

His lip trembled. I could sense the waterworks coming, but I didn't care. These kids needed some serious toughening up. No one would ever have caught me crying in public, not even at his age. How did the nuns expect the kids to survive out there in the big bad real world with such thin skins? Lucky for them, I was there to set things right with some much-needed tough love.

I tossed the kid's artwork aside. "Next!"

A girl came up, holding out a crayon drawing proudly. I inspected it for a second. "Trash!"

Nomfundo was next. She handed me her artwork.

I looked it over, then put on a cheerful voice. "Well now, look at this! Look at the patterns. Look at the colours..."

She beamed.

"Trash!" I declared. "Next!"

Nomfundo scowled at me. "You're Mister Meanie."

I shrugged. "Hey, life's tough, little girl. Get used to it."

But she didn't budge. She folded her arms and glared at me. "That's because you don't have any friends."

"Of course I have friends."

She shook her head. "No, you don't."

"Yes, I do!"

"Don't!"

"Do!"

Our debate was interrupted by a knock on the door. Sister Maria, Mandla and Ayanda entered without waiting for me to respond.

"Children, we have a visitor," Sister Maria announced. "The Mother Superior has come to visit us. Say hello!"

An elderly nun stepped into the room, smiling, and I was so shocked I nearly toppled out of my seat. She had aged significantly since I last saw her, but there was no doubt that I was looking at the one person in the orphanage who would recognise me, even after all these years. Sister Lucy. Well, Mother Superior now. I guess she had climbed the convent ladder.

The children greeted her in a chorus. "Hello Mother Superior."

Mother Superior's eyes scanned the room, and finally landed on me. Maybe her eyesight wasn't as strong as it used to be. Maybe I looked too suave in my new threads. Ah...nope. The minute she saw me she did a double take.

"Senzo Mabizela! Is that you?"

Damnit! There was no way to avoid her. I stumbled to my feet, thinking quickly. I stole a glance at Ayanda. She looked confused. I had to find a way out of this, or I'd be in big trouble. Mother Superior came over and wrapped me in a tight hug.

"Oh, thank God!" she murmured. "Senzo, my son. I thought I'd never see you again. Praise God!"

I tried to pull away, but damn, the woman still had an iron grip. "No, you're mistaken," I mumbled over her shoulder. "It's not me. I mean I'm not..."

She laughed, released me and then – to my horror – pinched my cheeks like I was still one of her charges. "Don't be silly," she said. "I'd know those cheeks anywhere. Are you still a naughty boy or have you become someone in life, my son? I haven't seen you since you left the orphanage –"

"What?" Ayanda looked from me to Mother Superior. "Orphanage?" Her eyes narrowed. "You mean *this* orphanage?"

I chuckled, trying to lighten the mood. It didn't work. Suddenly it was really hot in that classroom. I reached up to loosen my collar. "I don't know what she's talking about," I said with a shrug.

Mother Superior laughed again. At least one of us was having a good time. "Oh, Senzo! Still full of jokes. I'm glad to see that you still have that great sense of humour." She turned to face the others. "He used to come back to the orphanage after being bullied by the other kids and we'd talk and talk. He was my favourite because no matter how tough it got – and it got really tough sometimes – Senzo never lost his charm and sense of humour. That, they could never beat out of him." She touched my shoulder. "I'm really glad that you came back to the orphanage, that you never forgot your roots."

I had no idea what to say. I looked at Ayanda. Her lips were pursed and her eyes were cold. I swallowed. I'd seen her look at Jasper the same way, and I hated the idea of being lumped with that fool.

"Ayanda –" I began, but she cut me off.

"And that whole story about growing up in exile?"

"It's not what you think," I told her. "I can explain."

"No need to explain. Basically you were lying to me all along."

I cleared my throat. "Well, not quite. I just –"

"Oh, stuff it, Senzo," she snapped, and stormed out.

I saw Mandla grin, the bastard, but I had no time for him. I chased after Ayanda. I found her striding towards the gates. I caught up with her and grabbed her hand.

"Ayanda, I can explain!"

She pulled her hand away. "You lied to me! I don't even know who you are! And I trusted you with all of these children!"

"Let me explain," I blurted out. "It's true that I lied to you, and I'm sorry. I just felt so ashamed about where I really come from. I felt that I wasn't good enough because of my...my... my poor background."

She shook her head in disgust. "You ought to be ashamed of yourself!"

"Trust me, I am." I sighed. "But you don't know what it's like. How people look at you like you're beneath them! No one took me seriously when they heard where I came from, so I made up a different past."

She didn't respond, but at least she was still there, listening. If this was my only chance with her, I couldn't blow it. I'd have to tell the truth – or some of it, anyway.

"Don't give up on me, Ayanda," I pleaded. "I get these kids. I know where they're coming from. I'm one of them. I know how easy it is to judge, but try to understand. All I want, all I've ever wanted is for someone to love me. Someone to want to have me as a part of their life. Not out of pity, but just for who I am."

She softened. Still she said nothing, but I knew I had her full attention.

"Being an orphan wasn't easy," I went on. "But I shouldn't have lied about it. I promise I will never lie to you ever again. Give me another chance, please?"

She bit her lip, and tears came to her eyes.

"Please, Ayanda."

She took a deep breath, then took my hand and pulled me in for a hug. I couldn't believe it. I'd hoped for forgiveness, but I never imagined I'd get the chance to be that close to her, to hold her. My arms wrapped around her and I closed my eyes, breathing her in. She smelled amazing, of course. I smiled, savouring the moment.

6.

"Where the hell are you?"

I chuckled into the phone and peeled away from Ayanda, gesturing that I'd only be gone for a minute, then stepped into the corridor. "Calm down, Vus. It's a public holiday."

"Ja, the busiest day for Prophet Mazinga. We've already lost two customers!"

"I thought you'd be glad to have time to look for a real job," I replied coldly. "Hasn't Zanele hooked you up yet?"

He let out a weary sigh on the other end. "Senzo, if we don't work we don't get paid. I need to get paid! We're almost out of cash."

"I told you I had to be at the orphanage. It's important."

"So is making a living, man! Can you stop thinking with your –"

"Hey!" I snapped irritably. "You've been complaining about the Mazinga thing for ages, now you're worried about losing customers?" I lowered my voice to a whisper. "Just give me some time, okay? This will pay off, I promise."

"Ag, whatever," he replied, and hung up.

I made my way back towards the classroom, where Ayanda and the kids were waiting.

"Was that Vusi?" asked Ayanda.

I nodded. "He's so dependent on me, he gets nervous when I leave him alone."

"That's sweet," she said. "It's nice that you're so close." She glanced at her watch. "Oh, I need to go."

"Go where? I thought you were working here all day."

"I promised to drop off some papers for the lady who runs the legal clinic." She gave me a teasing smile. "I'll be back, don't worry."

"How's it going at the clinic, anyway?"

She picked her handbag off the desk. "Good. I haven't had much free time, but you'll never guess who offered to help."

"Who?"

"Jasper!"

My smile vanished. "Jasper?"

Ayanda nodded. "I'm always talking about the legal clinic but I didn't think he ever listened. Then yesterday I was in the office, chatting to our secretary about all these false prophet scams, and Jasper just jumped into the conversation. It was so strange. He seemed really interested, and then out of nowhere he offered to find out about the prophets here in the township."

That bastard!

"I think he's trying to impress me, but to be honest I need the help," she went on.

Before I could think of anything to say, my phone rang again.

"Busy man," Ayanda remarked with a grin.

I excused myself and stepped into the corridor again. The caller was Sipho, the "special case". I put on my Prophet Mazinga voice before answering.

"Some guy was asking for you at the shebeen," he reported.

I frowned. "Which guy?"

"I don't know, Prophet. He's not from around here."

The wheels started to turn in my head. "Expensive clothes, bad attitude?"

"Ja, you know him?" asked Sipho.

Ayanda emerged from the classroom. I waved as she went down the corridor. "Yes, I know him." After what Ayanda had just told me, I knew it had to be Jasper. "What did he want?"

"I don't know, he was just asking for Prophet Mazinga."

"When did this happen?"

"Just now. He came in and started asking for you. I told him you were not around, and he laughed at my voice." He clicked his tongue furiously.

"Sipho, what did you do?"

"Hey, I was going to leave him alone, but he couldn't shut his mouth. He called me ka_ _ _r!"

I gasped in shock. Surely not even Jasper would be that – no, he would.

"What was I supposed to do? Just leave it? No, my man, I taught him a lesson and I took his fancy wallet. He won't come back."

"You did what you had to do," I agreed, nodding my approval. "The ancestors would agree." I knew all about the kind of "lessons" Sipho liked to teach people. They were just like the "lessons" Jasper used to teach me back in school. How's that for karma?

"But he didn't leave by himself. One of the girls followed him. The troublesome one."

I was sure I already knew who he meant. There weren't many working girls who spent all their time at the shebeen, and only one of them was infamous for being a troublemaker.

"Sweets?"

"Ja," said Sipho. "That one."

My heart sank. It was bad enough that Jasper was sniffing around without Sweets adding to the mess. Two people who hated me, working together? Disaster.

"So how are you going to thank me?" Sipho went on.

"Eh? What do you mean?"

"The guy was going to make trouble for you and I fixed him. So let's talk. Maybe a discount for my treatment."

I sighed. I should have seen that coming. "I didn't ask you to beat him up."

"Oh, it's like that?" His voice had become even higher. That was a very bad sign. "Prophet, I always do what you say. I always help you. I took that lady's bag. I passed the test, isn't it? The ancestors say I am worthy!"

I should have known that little trick was going to come back to bite me. Sipho was a believer, but he also had a temper. "Sipho, look, it's fine. I'm grateful," I blurted out hastily. "Fifty per cent off."

"Free."

My jaw dropped. "That's three hundred bucks!"

"Ja, but the medicine doesn't work."

I rolled my eyes. "It's not my fault your manhood is beyond all help!"

"Hey, hey, hey," he said, with a trace of embarrassment. "I'm worthy, Prophet. You said so. Deal or no deal?"

I had no choice. A pissed-off Sipho could break me in half. "Okay. Okay. Deal."

"Sharp."

I hung up, feeling weary. I was getting too old for the hustle. With a sigh I stepped back into the classroom.

*

Spending the rest of the day with Ayanda was enough to chase away my blues, though. Later on we walked through the corridor, hand in hand. Yes, that's right – hand in hand. We didn't notice Mother Superior coming up behind us until she spoke.

"Senzo, can I talk to you?" We turned around to face her. She looked anxious. "In private? Ayanda, you don't mind do you?"

I minded. I don't know why no one thought to ask my opinion. I minded very much!

"Not at all," said Ayanda. "You'll find me with the kids."

I let go of her hand reluctantly. Once she was out of earshot, Mother Superior smiled and said, "She really likes you."

I beamed. So I wasn't imagining it, after all. "I feel like I've known her all my life."

The two of us walked down the passage together.

"I just wanted to say how proud of you I am," she said. "You turned out to be an outstanding and honest young man."

Ahem. Ja, neh. Honest. My smile faded slightly. Usually I lapped up that kind of praise, but since Ayanda and I had started spending time together, my less than immaculate track record had become a source of constant anxiety.

"What do you do for a living?"

Wow. The old lady was on a roll today with the tough questions.

I cleared my throat and told her the same thing I'd told Ayanda. "I'm an entrepreneur."

Mother Superior beamed proudly, and I felt a stab of guilt. "That is really impressive, Senzo. When I think of where you came from..." Tears sprang to her eyes, and when she spoke again she choked up. "I'm sure your mother really regrets abandoning you now."

Yes, my mother – what? I stopped and turned to face her. "My mother didn't abandon me." Mother Superior wasn't as young as she used to be; she must have mixed me up with one of the other orphanage kids. "My parents died. Remember?"

She dropped her gaze and took my hands in hers. Oh, no. This didn't look good at all. "That's what I tell all the children, Senzo," she said in a gentle voice. "I tell them that someday some kind person is going to come and take them in. I don't want them growing up feeling unloved and hopeless all their lives. But the truth is most of these kids at the orphanage have been abandoned. Like you."

It took a minute for me to process what she was saying. All those years...and here I thought nuns weren't supposed to lie. How could she not have told me? More importantly, if my mother hadn't died when I was a child, where the hell was she?

"So my mother is alive?" I asked. My voice was hoarse. "Somewhere out there?"

Mother Superior nodded.

"And she just left me?" I could feel it now, the bitterness. The shock had passed and now I felt the heat of rage. "How could she do that?"

"Life can be very difficult and it affects us all differently," said Mother Superior. "Just be grateful that things turned out so well for you in the end. It doesn't turn out that way for most people."

No, it didn't turn out well for most people, and it hadn't turned out well for me. I had been lost my whole childhood and now I was lost all over again.

"You should have told me," I said, pulling away from her.

She nodded. "I was going to, when you finished school. I thought you'd stay until matric but you left unexpectedly, before I had the chance."

There was a lot I could have said, but I didn't know where to begin. It had taken me a long time to come to terms with being an orphan, to stop comparing myself to kids whose parents still lived. I owned my tragedy eventually, and it became part of my foundation. Even in all my different incarnations – Senzo the child of exile, Prophet Mazinga – I was an orphan. It was the one thing about me that I couldn't fake, and now it turned out that it had never been real.

"I know who she is," she whispered. "I've always known. I was going to tell you everything, but –"

I stared at her in shock. "You know her?"

She nodded. "Senzo, it was complicated. I know right now it seems like a terrible betrayal, but so much happened before you were born. The man who – your father – he was not a kind person..." She stopped and took a deep breath. "Your mother went through a lot to keep you, to have you. She was so young and so scared. She couldn't be a mother. There was no one else. She couldn't do it so she came to us and we took you. But now you're a grown man and you deserve to know the woman who gave you life."

"I don't want to know," I blurted out.

"Senzo, please. Think about it."

"I don't want to think about it!" I shouted. "I don't want anything to do with her!"

I almost wished that Mother Superior had kept the truth to herself. What was the point of telling me now that my life story was a lie? What the hell was I supposed to do with that? I was hurt, angry and confused. I had to get out of that place.

I walked away without a word, brushing right past Ayanda. I heard her call my name, but I didn't answer. I needed to be alone.

*

Nomfundo was the one who found me some time later. I was sitting in the playground, staring into space and trying to make sense of things. She came and sat beside me without an invitation.

"You look sad," she said.

I didn't answer. I was in no mood for company.

"It's okay," she decided, leaning against me. "I'll be your friend."

I resisted for a minute, but eventually the kid wore me down. She was being so sweet, I had to respond. "I just got some very sad news."

Nomfundo moved away and looked up at me. "Do you want to talk about it?"

"No."

"Okay." She folded her hands, waiting. I knew this game, and Nomfundo was good at it. She could sit there forever.

"Okay, okay." I sighed. "You know I used to be – well, I guess I still am – an orphan. Well, not really. I don't know..."

"Wow, you're all mixed up."

"Yes. Yes, I am." I took a deep breath. "I just found out that my mother is still alive. That means she abandoned me." There. I had said it and I couldn't take it back. It was out there. It was real. "She's not dead. She just didn't want me."

After a brief silence Nomfundo said, "I know my mommy also abandoned me. Even though Sister Maria says she didn't."

I looked at the kid in surprise. "You do? Then... But... How do you handle it? Doesn't it make you sad?"

She nodded. "Sometimes. But I don't think about it. I look after other people, and then they become my family."

I digested this precocious statement for a while. I had always known that living in the orphanage forced kids to grow up quickly. It had never occurred to me that it could also make them wise.

Nomfundo got up to leave. "I'm going back inside now."

"Have you finished your homework?"

"No, not yet."

I hesitated. "Do you want me to help you with it?"

Her face lit up with excitement. "Yes please!"

I got to my feet, glad to have a distraction. "Come on, let's go."

A few minutes later I was walking around the classroom, inspecting all the children's homework. I stopped to admire a picture one of the boys was drawing.

"That's good," I told him.

He looked at me in surprise. "Really?"

I nodded, and he beamed. I walked around to a girl busy doing some sums.

"Ten times ten is a hundred," I said, reading over her shoulder. "Well done!"

I have to say, it made me feel good to say nice things to the kids. For the first time I looked at them and saw myself. A lot of them would grow up just the way I did, thinking their parents were dead when they weren't. They might grow up to be naughty. Some might even grow up to be con artists, or thieves, or gangsters.

I had been in the scam game a long, long time, and it was rare for me to feel guilty. A man had to do what was necessary to survive, right? At least that was what I told myself. I never took money from people who had less than me, only from the lucky ones with jobs and insecurities. But how could I be sure? It's not like I ever did a background check. How did I know my clients weren't spending their last cent on some treatment that would never work?

Yoh, the guilt was heavy. No wonder I had never allowed myself to feel it before. It sat in my chest, making it hard to breathe. I looked around the classroom. They were just kids. Sure, they were annoying and loud and forward, but I had probably been like that too. They were lost, like me, without families to keep them grounded.

Then I noticed that the kids were all staring at me. I cleared my throat. "What's wrong? Why have you stopped working?"

"Are you angry with us?" one of them asked. "We don't like it when you're angry."

Shit. Suddenly there was a lump in my throat. "I'm not angry. You're all doing great today. Keep it up." I tried to smile, but it was hard. There were too many conflicting emotions inside me.

Out of nowhere a little girl came up to me and wrapped her arms around my legs. At first I was too shocked to move or speak. Slowly I leaned down to pat her head. Next thing I knew another kid had come to join the party, and another, and another, until there were a whole lot of little arms wrapped in a huge group hug. I felt a lot of things – confused, angry, sad – but I also felt all warm and fuzzy inside. No, really. I did. And though I would deny it if anyone ever brought it up, I might even have shed a tear.

*

That night Ayanda dropped me off a good distance from the consulting room. I made her park near some nice flats. I would have lived there if I made more money, so it was only a half-lie.

"Thanks for the lift," I said as the car came to a stop at the side of the road.

"No problem," she replied. "How they can refuse to give you a courtesy car when you took your car in for service is beyond me, hey."

Ahem. Okay, so maybe I had told a few more half-lies. Maybe a couple of full lies as well. There were worse crimes.

I shrugged. "I left it alone. I didn't want to get anyone fired or anything."

Ayanda smiled. "You're really sweet sometimes, you know that? I think that's why the kids like you so much."

No, it was because I was as lonely as they were. "I just have a lot in common with them."

She reached out and touched my hand. I looked into her eyes and I knew we both felt the chemistry.

"Listen," she said softly, "about what Mother Superior told you... You don't have to share if you don't want to, but I want you to know that I'm here if you need to talk."

I didn't answer.

"Senzo? Are you okay?"

I took a deep breath, and before I knew it the words were pouring out. She already knew I grew up in the orphanage, so I might as well tell her the rest. "It turns out I'm not an orphan after all. My mother didn't die, she gave me up. Sister Lucy – I mean Mother Superior – said she was very young when she had me. Something bad happened with my father. I don't know, maybe he abused her. But my mother couldn't look after me, so she gave me to the nuns."

Ayanda took my hand and squeezed it. "I'm sorry. It must have been such a shock to hear that after all this time."

"That's not even the worst part." I shook my head, still trying to make sense of the facts. "She's out there, somewhere in the township, right now. My mother. She's been living right under my nose all this time. The nuns knew who she was and they never told me! Can you believe it? Mother Superior said she was waiting to tell me when I finished school, but I left the orphanage and never went back."

"I'm sure she was just doing what she thought was best," said Ayanda.

"She should have told me long ago!"

"She was going to. Senzo, I don't know anything about your situation, but I know one thing for sure. The nuns love their kids, and everything they do is out of love and concern. I'm sure Mother Superior was trying to protect you."

"Maybe."

But I was still angry. Maybe my mother couldn't deal with raising me at first, but what about later? She could have at least come back when she was older, when she could handle it. How could she leave me alone for so long? I probably had relatives I knew nothing about, grandparents, cousins, aunts and uncles. People who would have looked out for me. She deprived me of all that.

"Did Mother Superior tell you who your mother is?" asked Ayanda.

I shook my head. "I don't want to know."

"I don't believe that," she replied gently. "You're angry right now, but deep down you must want to know. You must have so many questions."

I groaned. "I don't want to talk about this anymore."

Ayanda nodded. "Okay." She leaned over to hug me.

She was warm and still smelled wonderful, even after a long day of work. For those few moments I felt better. Then she let go, and all the bad feelings came rushing back.

"What are you doing tomorrow morning?" she asked.

I shrugged. "Nothing much."

"Don't just say that to be accommodating." She smiled. "I know entrepreneurs are some of the busiest people. You know, you never told me what kind of business you run."

Oh, ja. With all the drama around my mother I had forgotten that I was supposed to be a self-made man. "It's a marketing and brand management company, but I actually just sold it. I prefer to set up a company and sell it off so I can spend more time doing community work." The lies slid right off my tongue. I was getting so good at it I was starting to freak myself out. "I'm planning to set up a new venture soon, but for now I still have some free time. Why, what's up?"

"Me and Mandla are playing tennis in the morning. I was thinking maybe you and Vusi..."

"I'd love to." Vusi wouldn't be thrilled, but I could find a way around that.

Ayanda grinned. "Awesome. Then it's a date. See you at nine."

"Nine it is. SMS me the address. I'll get a ride with Vus," I added as an afterthought.

Ayanda frowned. "How does Vusi have a car? Didn't you only find him a job recently?"

Oops. I had forgotten that Vusi was a reformed hobo. It was hard to remember all my stories. "It was a gift. You know, to make it easier for him to move around town."

"That's incredible, Senzo." She shook her head, amazed by my generosity. "Well, see you tomorrow."

"Thanks for the invite."

"You're welcome."

Neither of us moved for a moment. I was so tempted to kiss her, but I wasn't sure how she'd react. Eventually I smiled, opened the door and climbed out of the car. I waited until she had driven off before turning and walking in the opposite direction, towards the consulting room. Damnit, the lies were starting to trip me up. I had to be more careful.

The consulting room was unlocked and the lights were on. Vusi must be in. I walked in and froze. The room was a disaster. Our things were thrown across the floor, the mat was crumpled, and Vusi stood in a corner of the room, scanning the mess.

"Shit!" I gasped. "What happened? Were we robbed?"

"There's nothing worth stealing in here," Vusi reminded me. "I saw Jasper hanging around here earlier. He tried to follow me but I shook him off."

I closed my eyes. Damnit! I had forgotten all about Jasper. After what Sipho had told me earlier, there was no doubt that it was Jasper who had ransacked the place. "Yes, it was him. Sipho called to tell me Jasper had been at the shebeen."

Vusi's eyes widened. "*Our* shebeen? Not a bar in Sandton?"

"He wouldn't have found Prophet Mazinga in Sandton." I picked my way through the mess. "Apparently he was asking about me – Mazinga – and he made the mistake of making fun of Sipho's voice."

"Ooh, bad move."

"Exactly. He got himself beaten up." I sighed, surveying the damage. "Sipho said Jasper left with Sweets."

Vusi groaned. "Your two worst enemies! That woman would sell us out for a pack of cigarettes."

"Ja, but even if she told him about the scam, he has no proof. Unless..." I spotted a half-open drawer and moved to check inside. It was empty. I looked around on the floor, but there was no sign of the photo of me and Vusi in our sangoma gear. We had taken it in the early days, before we perfected the con. Let's just say the disguises weren't very effective back then.

"He's taken the photo," I told Vusi.

"I told you not to keep that thing!" he exclaimed. "I told you it would get us busted, and what did you say? You said we needed to remember how far we had come. You said no one would care about a stupid photo. Just like you said no one would go to the papers, and look what happened last year."

"Ja, okay, Vus," I said impatiently. "I screwed up. The point is we may have to lay low for a while."

"But where do we go?"

I sighed, suddenly feeling exhausted. It had been a long day. "I don't know. I'm so tired of all this lying and pretending and stuff." I flopped onto the couch. "I want to come clean with Ayanda. With everyone actually. My whole life has been a lie! I don't want to go on living this way."

Vusi sat beside me. "Bra, you know I want to give up the scam, but Ayanda will never forgive you for lying to her. Trust me on that one."

"She already knows about the orphanage. Sister Lucy was there today and she recognised me." I told him all about what happened, including the news about my mother.

"Sorry, bra," he said. "Eish. Life, neh?"

"Ja. Life."

We sat in silence for a few minutes, digesting everything that had happened.

"I still think I should tell Ayanda," I said. "She was so understanding about the thing with my mother."

"Ja, because you're the victim," Vusi pointed out. "Anyone with a heart would feel bad for you. But all the lies you told her? About having a lot of money, running your own business, saving me from the streets? That's another story."

He was right, but I thought about the way Ayanda had squeezed my hand and hugged me, and the look in her eye when she said goodnight. She cared about me.

"She invited us to play tennis with her tomorrow. I'll talk to her after that." I got to my feet. "I'm going home."

"Wait!" said Vusi, jumping up to follow me. "Jasper could still be out there. And since when do we play tennis?"

7.

I didn't tell Ayanda the truth after all. Big surprise, right? Look, I wanted to. Really. But it was hard to find the right moment.

We played doubles, me with Ayanda and Mandla with Vusi. Me and Ayanda wiped the floor with Vusi and Mandla, to my surprise. I guess I was a natural at tennis, despite always thinking it was boring. We had Mandla and Vusi running all over the court and falling over themselves to reach the balls. It was hilarious. At one point – or maybe several points – the ball smacked right into Vusi's head. I didn't want to laugh at my boy, but man, it was funny.

After that there was no time to talk to Ayanda. We got changed and we all walked out together. Really, it was the most inconvenient set-up for making a confession, and despite my noble intentions I had to accept that the timing was all wrong. Besides, Vusi was right. Women hated being lied to. Ayanda and I had really bonded over my sad childhood, and I didn't want to do anything to spoil it. That meant I had to keep playing the game.

As we walked into the parking lot I picked an expensive car at random and lingered next to it. Vusi joined me, and the two of us dropped our bags. Vusi bent over, pretending to do his laces.

Ayanda turned to face us. "So we're on for tonight, hey?"

I grinned. "Ja. Where am I taking you?"

"How about..." She smiled. "You know the chisa nyama close to the orphanage? I've always wanted to check it out."

Beautiful, sophisticated, smart, kind *and* down to earth. Ayanda was a keeper for sure. "Deal! Chisa nyama it is."

She leaned over to give me a peck on the cheek.

"Can we go already?" said Mandla. The guy really didn't like me. I had made an effort not to wear blue and brown again, but apparently that wasn't enough.

Ayanda and Mandla headed towards their car. We watched, waving until the car peeled off. A burly man stepped out of the tennis club, fiddling with his car keys. The car we were lounging on unlocked with a beep-beep, and we jumped off. The guy shot us a suspicious look, and we picked up our bags and hurried away.

"That was close!" said Vusi.

"Ja."

I felt that unpleasant pang of guilt again. What was wrong with me? Ever since I found Ayanda I had suddenly developed a conscience, and it was a serious pain in the butt. I needed to be sharp, carefree Senzo again, the Senzo who hustled and got things done.

I pushed the guilt away. Life was hard for a guy like me, and there was no time to feel bad. I had three clients lined up for the day and I had to do what I had to do. A clear conscience wasn't going to put food in my belly or pay my rent, and it certainly wasn't going to win over the woman of my dreams. I had to play the game and win.

*

That night Ayanda and I sat at one of the tables outside the chisa nyama. The sun was setting as we gazed into each other's eyes, oblivious of the laughter and chatter around us.

"This is so chilled," said Ayanda, with a contented sigh. "Thanks, Senzo. Jasper would never bring me here. He can be so pretentious sometimes."

"Then why date him?" I asked. "That's if you are still dating him."

"We're on a break," she said. "Jasper is...complex. He was very charming at first. And very persistent. And my dad adores him. You know, sometimes you find yourself in a situation that you can't get out of," she added cryptically. "And after a while it's hard to leave because it's become...well..."

"Like a habit?"

She smiled at me. "Yes, exactly. Better the devil you know."

"I get it."

"Do you?" she asked in a teasing tone. "You also have a complicated love life?"

"Life in general is complicated," I told her. "We all do things we can't explain to other people. You do what you can to survive, right?"

"I suppose that's one way of looking at it." She ate with her hands, like a real woman, enjoying her food. I liked watching her eat. I liked watching her, full stop. Being with her took my mind off all the other drama in my life.

"You never talk about your mother," I remarked.

Ayanda shrugged. "She died when I was young. My dad tried hard to be there for me, but he was always working."

"Sounds lonely. At least in the orphanage I had other kids around me all the time."

"It *was* lonely." She looked sad for a minute. "I had to learn to be independent from a young age. But my father is also the reason I have such a strong work ethic. I knew that I had to make him proud."

"And now you're a beautiful, successful, brilliant lawyer," I said. "He must be *very* proud."

She smiled. "Thank you. You turned out pretty well yourself. It's amazing how far you've come, considering your childhood. If your mother knew you, she'd be proud too."

My heart sank. Ag, she just had to go and bring that up, when we were having such a great time.

"Have you thought about meeting her?"

"Why should I?" I snapped, suddenly angry again. "If she wanted to know me she would come looking for me. Why should I go chasing someone who doesn't care?"

"You know it's not that simple, Senzo." Ayanda arched her brows. "You can't tell me you haven't wondered about her."

I leaned back in the chair. "Of course I have. Look, I want to know a lot of things. I want to know why she abandoned me, why she never came back. Maybe one day I'll go and find her, but I'm too angry with her to do anything right now."

Ayanda nodded. "I understand. Well, whatever you decide, I'm here to support you." She smiled, and I smiled back. Then her smile vanished. She leaned her head to the left, staring past me. "Either the light's playing tricks on me or that guy's naked."

I chuckled, but didn't bother to turn around. "That's nothing. I've seen worse around here."

"There's something familiar about him,'" she persisted. "He sort of looks like Jasper."

"Then the light *is* playing tricks on you," I assured her. I took her hands in mine. "Ayanda, there's something I've been meaning to tell you."

I had her full attention once again. "What?"

"I...I'm really happy that I met you and I..." I took a deep breath.

"You what?" She was smiling, and I knew she wanted me to make a move.

The opportunity was right there, so I took it. I let the moment linger, then leaned in for a kiss. She leaned in too, closing her eyes. Our lips were just about to touch when –

"Don't kiss that guy!"

We sprang apart and turned to stare at the owner of the familiar voice. It was Jasper. He stood a few steps away from us, panting, clutching a newspaper and wearing nothing but his underwear. Shit.

"Jas-Jasper?" Ayanda gasped. "What happened?"

He pointed at me, his eyes wild with fury. "He's an impostor!"

My stomach started to twist with fear. Oh, no. Not now. Not when everything was going so well with Ayanda! Two waiters appeared instantly and moved towards Jasper, like special agents closing in on a terrorist.

"What are you talking about?" I demanded. I was proud of myself – my voice only trembled slightly.

"You're not a former exile," Jasper sneered.

"She already knows that," I told him smugly. "So if you're here to cause trouble –"

"You're not wealthy, either," he went on. "And you're definitely not a prophet!"

"Prophet?" Ayanda stared at Jasper, then at me. "What prophet? Who said he's a prophet?"

"Sir, I'm afraid we're going to have to ask you to leave," said one of the waiters, taking hold of Jasper's shoulder. By now he had attracted shocked stares and giggles from the other customers.

Jasper shrugged the waiter off. "Get your hands off of me! Do you know who I am?"

"Sorry, sir," said the second waiter. "We have a dress code. You can't just come in here in your underwear." The waiters lunged. There was a brief tussle.

"These are designer undies!" Jasper yelled. "I'm going to sue all of you! And I can afford it!"

"Throw him out," I called out. "Designer undies. Sies!"

"Stop!" cried Ayanda, with a disapproving glance in my direction. "I know him."

The waiters backed off. Panting, Jasper handed Ayanda the newspaper.

"What's this?" she asked.

I closed my eyes, praying that the newspaper wasn't what I thought it was.

"You wanted information on the false prophets in the township," he told her. "Well, there's the biggest fraud of all. Your boyfriend, Senzo. If that's even his real name."

I opened my eyes again. So much for that prayer. Ayanda took the newspaper and looked at the front page. It was the article that had exposed the Mazinga scam over a year earlier, the handiwork of a disgruntled client and his journalist cousin. There was even a photo of me, in my wig but without the shades, and Vusi emerging from our first consulting room and walking right into a camera. We both looked shocked and very, very guilty.

I would never forget the headline: "False Prophet Busted... Mazinga Steals From The Poor". Our clients were not poor, they were just not rich. The article appeared in a cheap tabloid and the police didn't bother investigating, but me and Vusi packed up and moved shop anyway. We didn't work the scam for five months, just to be safe. Fortunately scandal had a short shelf life in Jozi, and soon enough people forgot. Besides, there would always be a market for what Prophet Mazinga sold.

There was only one person I knew who would still have a newspaper from over a year ago. Jaklas, an old kasi hobo who liked to play dice. He kept piles and piles of newspapers. He wrapped them carefully with plastic as if they were his most valuable belongings, and no one knew why. He would do anything for a game of a dice, even give away one of his precious newspapers. That had to be how Jasper got it, and Sweets must have helped.

I looked at the horrified expression on Ayanda's face, and I knew it was all over.

"He's been lying to you all along!" said Jasper gleefully. "He's not who he says he is. He's a con-man from the township. A false prophet!"

Ayanda looked up from the newspaper and turned to me. "Is it true?"

"I can explain..." I began, and I realised how sick I was of all the lies. It was time for the truth. The whole truth. "Actually I can't. It's true. I've been lying to you all along."

Tears welled up in Ayanda's eyes. I reached for her hand. She pulled away and slapped me hard across the face, then picked up her purse and stormed off towards her car. I sat there with my head buried in my hands, while Jasper ran after Ayanda, begging her to wait for him.

I sensed someone beside me and looked up, hoping...but it was just the waiter. He placed a tall glass of beer on the table in front of me, gave me a pitying look and said, "On the house."

After drinking my beer I walked home. A few people called out to me but I didn't answer. I was in no mood to be happy, cheerful Senzo Mabizela now that I had lost the woman of my dreams. On the way I passed the spot where Jaklas liked to sit and play dice. He was still there, sitting on an overturned crate and carefully putting fresh plastic over another stack of newspapers.

"Sure, Jaklas," I said as I passed.

"Mabizela! Sit down, sit down." Jaklas patted the crate next to him. "Let's play."

I wanted to refuse, but this was the place where Jasper had found the newspaper that ruined my life. Maybe it would help to find out exactly what happened between him and Jaklas. Besides, what else did I have going on? Vusi and Zanele were probably curled up together at the flat and the last thing I wanted was to be around a happy couple.

"You go first," I said, sitting on the crate.

Jaklas picked up his grimy dice and rolled. Eight. He chuckled and looked at me. I rolled next. Five. Jaklas laughed loudly.

"Too bad, too bad!" he shouted, rolling again.

By the time I finally scored higher than him I had lost thirty bucks and three cigarettes. He grumbled under his breath when I got double sixes. The guy was a sore loser, even though he only lost once in a blue moon.

He picked up the pack of mageu at his feet and opened it slowly with long, dirty fingernails. "Ja, fine. What do you want?" he demanded.

I leaned close and lowered my voice. "There was a guy here earlier. A rich guy."

Jaklas nodded. "Ja. Nice shirt. Nice belt. Nice shoes." He cackled.

"What did he want?"

Jaklas pointed at his stack of newspapers.

I nodded. "So what happened? Did he ask you anything about me? Was he with a woman?"

Jaklas took a loud gulp of mageu, wiped his lips on his sleeve and gave me a sly look. "Play again."

"Ag, come on." I emptied my pockets to show him I had nothing more to give except my phone and some coins for transport. "I'm broke!"

"Broke se voet," he replied. "New question, new game."

I weighed my options. I was still upset about the money he had already won from me and I didn't feel like giving him any more. I already knew the important facts – Jaklas was the one who gave Jasper the paper with the article on Prophet Mazinga – and I was sure I could guess the rest. I started to get up.

"Ah, Mabizela! You're going?"

"Ja. I have things to do."

"Sit. Sit, sit. We play again." He picked up the dice. "One round, neh? Or three. Just three."

I shook my head.

"I'll tell you what happened with your rich friend," he promised. "Sit. Five rounds only, and I'll tell you."

Huh, this guy thought I was a domkop. Already we had gone from one more round to five. "Just five?"

"Ten. Ten rounds."

I couldn't help laughing. Ag, what did I have to lose? It was better than going home to cry into my pillow or something. (Not that I would. I'm not a baby.) The poor guy didn't have any family or friends, and he was probably just lonely. It wouldn't hurt to sit and play with him a while longer and let him tell me exactly how he managed to strip Jasper of all his designer clothes.

I sat down.

"Ja, bra, good!" He smacked his lips with pleasure. "Start."

I rolled the dice. Three. Jaklas laughed loudly, slapping his knees like it was the funniest thing in the world. For a minute I thought he might backtrack and refuse to tell me about Jasper – that would be so typical – but he didn't. He told me the whole story, laughing like a hyena throughout.

"Ah, your friend," he said, shaking his head. "Rich and stupid. Up here," he tapped his head, "empty. That girl brings him. You know the one?" He mimed an hourglass figure and wolf whistled for good measure. "Then she goes. Leaves him. He comes with his fancy clothes, asking questions. I just ignore. He sees the newspaper and he wants to take it. Ha-ah! Just like that! You know what I tell him? Me, I say we must play. He starts talking kak. I say hey, no game no paper!" He burst out laughing. Kwa-kwa-kwa, like some kind of freaky bird.

I smiled. "And then?"

"Hoo, he sits down, he thinks he's Mr Cool, neh? I say, hmm, nice jacket. I win, I take. He laughs. Me, I say okay, we will see. And I beat him." Jaklas snapped his fingers. "He starts talking kak again. I say okay, I beat you again, I take that jacket. We play. I win. I take it! Hahahaha!"

I cracked up, picturing Jasper's furious expression. He must have thought he was too smart to get whipped by a hobo. Ha! I wish I had been there to see it for myself.

"So now he's angry, neh?" said Jaklas getting excited at the memory. "He's serious, wants to win back the jacket. I say hmm, nice belt. So we play. I win."

"And then you say hmm, nice pants," I said. We laughed together, enjoying the joke.

"Ja! Hahaha! We play again. I still win! Hoo! Until he's sitting in his boxer shorts and socks. And then, last game..." Jaklas sighed. "He wins. So I give him the newspaper. He tries to take my clothes and I hit him with my sjambok. Mxm! Stupid rich boy."

We laughed some more, and then Jaklas started all over again, as if he had never told the story before. And I listened. And I laughed. I laughed so hard tears poured down my face, like I hadn't laughed in a long, long time. I guess I needed to do that after the day I had. I needed to let loose and pretend I was still a carefree kid with no real worries.

I looked at Jaklas and realised that maybe I shouldn't feel sorry for him. Jaklas lived a simple life. He had his precious newspapers and his shopping trolley filled with clothes and other items. Somehow he always found food to eat and a place to sleep. He had some tough gangster friends who brought him old clothes and cigarettes, and he spent all day doing the only things he wanted to do – playing dice and telling stories. He had nothing compared to Jasper, but I was pretty sure he was far happier than Jasper would ever be.

After we had played more than twenty rounds and I couldn't laugh anymore, I said bye to Jaklas, gave him my transport money and took a long walk home.

8.

"Love is a waste of time," I declared. "Look at you now. You're miserable. You're a mess. Finished. You really want more of that?"

The client blinked, confused. "But isn't it that true love always wins?"

I burst out into a fit of hysterical laughter. "Where did you hear such bullshit?" I leaned forward on the mat. "Let me tell you, my brother, in the real world love means nothing. I don't even think there is such a thing as love."

The client processed this for a minute. He was a middle-aged man, not very bright, but then again if he had been bright he wouldn't have been in my consulting room. "You're saying me and my wife are not in love?"

I shrugged. "From your story it sounds like you loved her but she loved your money, my friend."

He shook his head, still clinging to false hope. "But she didn't know I had money when we met. I only got it when my uncle died!"

"Oh, but she knew!" I assured him. "Women can sniff these things out. Now you're broke, she's tossed you to the side. She's probably with another man as we speak."

"Eh?"

I nodded. "Your wife is a lying gold-digger."

Suddenly the man lunged at me, grabbed me by the throat and started choking me. Vusi emerged from behind the curtain and pulled the madman off me.

"Hey, I'll kill you," the man snarled. "Give me back my money!"

"Forget it," said Vusi. "Get out of here." He tossed him out the door, slammed it shut and turned to me. "What the hell were you doing? Are you trying to ruin our business?"

I lay on my back on the mat. "What's the point, Vus? What's the meaning of life?"

"You're the prophet," said Vusi. "You tell me."

But I couldn't. I had no idea.

He sat beside me on the mat. "You know, you still have a way to get back at Jasper. You can tell Ayanda about him and Chairman, and about the cheating."

"Ayanda won't speak to me," I whispered miserably. "And even if she did, she wouldn't believe me."

Vusi sighed. "Why don't you go to the orphanage? You said you liked helping out. At least you can be useful there."

"What if Ayanda's there?"

"Maybe you can talk. Work it out. Maybe she is just waiting for you to try again."

I had to hand it to Vusi, he was a better bullshitter than I ever was. But it was what I wanted to hear. What I wanted to believe.

I got up and turned to him. "You're right. I'm going to the orphanage. And if I see her, I see her." I started towards the door.

"Er, Senzo?"

"Ja?"

"You're still wearing your wig."

"Oh, shit!"

*

I could hear her reading to the children as I walked up to the classroom door. I took a deep breath, knocked and entered. Ayanda looked up. There was a moment of eye contact, and then she looked away and snapped the book shut.

"Look, children. Uncle Senzo is here." I could tell that her cheerful voice was just a front. I was the last person she wanted to see.

"Hi, Uncle Senzo," the children chorused.

Even though I felt like I'd been punched in the stomach, I smiled and waved at them, then sat down on one of the kiddie chairs.

Ayanda got to her feet. "Now that Uncle Senzo is here, he can finish reading the story for you." She walked past me and dropped the book in my lap.

"Aya, I – "

She marched to the door and slammed it shut behind her. Ouch.

"Read us the story, Uncle Senzo," said Nomfundo.

With a weary sigh I got up and went to sit at the front of the class. "Okay, where were you?"

"The part about the ogre."

I scanned through the page. "Ah, here we are. So she said to her children, 'Children - you need to go and ask the ogre for food.'"

"No, I don't like that story," said Nomfundo. "It's going to end sadly. I just know it."

I shrugged and closed the book. It made no difference to me. "Okay. Suit yourself. Everyone go to sleep, then."

The other kids got ready for their naps, but Nomfundo came up to me. "Why did Aunty Ayanda leave?" she asked.

"I don't know."

"Why are you so sad?"

Damnit, the kid was too perceptive. "Who says I'm sad? I'm not sad, look." I forced a grin.

She wasn't convinced. "You know what I read when I am sad?" She opened up her pencil case and pulled out a folded, yellowing piece of paper. She handed it to me. "Here. Read it."

"No, you read it," I replied. "You need to practise.

"Okay." She started reading aloud. "There is so much I want to share with you, but my words are lost within me..."

Wait a minute. I stared at her in disbelief. I knew those words!

"I have so many emo... emo..."

"Emotions," I said.

"Emotions. How do I make you see?"

I couldn't believe it. I hadn't seen that poem in fifteen years, not since I crumpled it up and tossed it in the bin. How did Nomfundo get her hands on it? I began saying the words as she read them.

"Life is not that simple. Hear this from my heart. Our love will con-quer all, as we stand here at the start. Not speaking to you is killing me, you there and me here. But one day soon that will change..." She looked up, surprised. "Hey! You know the words."

"And I will finally have you near," I went on. "But now I stand here and wonder, if I will ever have you..."

"Ayanda!" cried Nomfundo. "How come you know it?"

"Who gave this to you?" I asked.

"Aunty Ayanda let me borrow it for a while. She told me it was her first love poem."

I gazed at the yellowing paper, at my handwriting. Ayanda must have taken the poem from the bin after I ran out of the classroom that day, and she had kept it all these years. What did that mean? I didn't know, but I had to find out.

I left the children napping and went to find Ayanda. I saw her stepping out of Sister Maria's office.

"Ayanda –"

She pushed past me and carried on walking.

"Wait. Aya, can we please–"

"No, we can't," she snapped, turning around to face me. "I have nothing to say to you, Senzo. And by the way, only my friends call me Aya." She stormed off once again.

Well, I had my answer. No matter how she felt about fourteen-year-old Senzo, Ayanda would never forgive the grown up version.

*

I returned to the consulting room to find the most unlikely person waiting for me. Mandla.

"What are you doing here?" I asked.

"I need your help," he told me. "I'm in love with Ayanda."

I laughed, until I saw the distraught expression on his face and realised he was serious. "Aren't you gay?"

He sighed. "No, I only pretended to be gay so that I could get close to her, but now my entire plan has backfired because I told her how I felt and she's angry and hurt that I lied to her, so now she's back with Jasper and honestly I would rather see her with you than with that arrogant, lowlife leech!"

Wow. It took me a moment to make sense of that speech. I let him in and the two of us sat down. There was a long awkward silence.

"Why are you telling me all this?" I asked finally.

"Because I know you hate Jasper as much as I do," said Mandla. "We need to find a way to take him down!"

I thought for a minute, and then I made a decision. "Actually," I said slowly, "I know something..."

*

"They're here!" Mandla whispered from the window. "Jasper's car has just pulled up outside."

The two of us were in Ayanda's apartment, courtesy of Mandla's spare key. I was pretty sure she had forgotten to take the key back once she found out her BFF was after the same thing as all the other men, and she wouldn't be thrilled to find us there. But I always liked to make a splash, and this time I had noble intentions for a change.

"Move away from the window before they see you," I told Mandla.

He came over and we stood waiting in the lounge. I could hear voices from outside.

"It would have been totally ungentlemanly of me to not walk you up to your door," Jasper was saying. I rolled my eyes. Gentlemanly, my foot.

"Thanks, I appreciate it," said Ayanda, unlocking the door.

"I mean, this is Jozi. Anything can happen between your car and your door –"

Ayanda spotted us standing there in the dark and shrieked.

Jasper screamed and fell to his knees. "Please don't hurt me!" And then – I could hardly believe it – he pushed Ayanda forward and cowered behind her!

For a moment we all stood there, shocked.

"You need to man up, bra," said Mandla in disgust.

He and I stepped into the light. Jasper got up, embarrassed, and dusted off his pants.

Ayanda glared at us. "You scared me to death! How the hell did you two get in here?"

"You gave me a set of keys," Mandla reminded her.

"You do know that trespassing is a crime, right?" Jasper snarled. "And in this part of town, they tend to take criminal activity very seriously!"

"Shut up," I snapped back. "We're here because Ayanda deserves to know the truth. All of us claim to care and yet we've lied to her, and it stops now. Ayanda, we're going to confess everything, and then you can decide whether to forgive us or not."

"This is the most –" Jasper began, but Ayanda held up her hand to shut him up.

"I'm listening," she said, folding her arms. "Since you've made such a dramatic entrance, I might as well let you say your piece."

So we told her. Mandla went first, explaining how he had pretended to be gay to get close to her. When he was done he heaved a sigh of relief and turned to me.

I took a deep breath. "I'm broke. I don't like kids. I've never built any schools in KZN. I lied to you so I could get closer to you and get you to like me. You probably don't remember, but the first time we met was in the ninth grade. You guys came to my school on a field trip."

Jasper gasped. "Yes! I remember! Mr. Poetry. Still a loser after all these –"

"Shut up, Jasper," said Mandla.

"Ever since that day, I've been in love with you, Ayanda," I went on. "Not one day has gone by without me thinking about you. And when I saw you again I was ready to do anything to impress you. So I got someone to steal your bag so I could bring it back and be the hero."

Her mouth dropped open.

"I know," I said with a sigh. "Believe me, I know. I've done a lot of crazy things. Pretending to be someone else, tricking people to get what I wanted. But being with you changed me. I've always had to hustle to get by. That was the only life I knew. Then you came along and I wanted to be a different person. A better person. I didn't know how, so I faked it. Now I realise that lying was the worst thing I could have done, and I'm truly sorry. That's the truth." I looked at Jasper. "Your turn."

There was a long silence. Ayanda turned to Jasper expectantly.

"Go on Jasper," I said. "Tell her how we met."

"What does that mean?" asked Ayanda. "Didn't you meet at the charity event?"

"It started with me handing you one of my flyers in traffic," I reminded him. "Prophet Mazinga from Mozambique. Remember? See your enemies in a mirror, penis enlargement, bring back lost lover."

Jasper's eyes narrowed, and I realised that this was the first time he recognised me as the guy from the traffic lights. We all waited for him to make his confession. He looked at Ayanda and took her hands in his.

"Yes, he gave me that stupid flyer, but I didn't even look at his face. I wish I had, then I would have been able to expose him sooner. I knew he looked familiar." He smiled at her. "Baby, *I* have never lied to you. I'm the only man here who can say that. I love you and I know you deserve better."

Mandla coughed and spluttered something that sounded like "Chairman." I looked on, both shocked and somewhat impressed by Jasper's utter lack of shame. Only a sociopath could keep lying at this point.

"I'm not like these lowlifes," he went on passionately. "You and I are cut from the same cloth babe, we know how to treat people with the respect they deserve."

Okay, that was enough. "That's a lie!" I blurted out. "Jasper came to me to –"

"Came to you for what?" he sneered. "What could I possibly want from the likes of you?"

Mandla snarled and took a step towards Jasper. "You lying two-faced son of –"

"Enough!" cried Ayanda.

"She's right. We should leave."

To my surprise, the calm voice of reason was my own. I had come to a realisation. Revealing Jasper's deceit wasn't going to change anything. He would simply lie his way out of it, and we had no proof. Besides, Ayanda knew Jasper was a jackass. If she wanted to spend the rest of her life with someone like him, that was her choice.

I turned to Ayanda. "We've put you through enough. I understand if you never want to see me again, but since I started working with the kids I realized that they mean a lot to me. I'm going to keep working there. I'll stay out of your way so we'll never have to meet, but I hope everything goes well for you." I shot a look at Jasper. "And I truly mean that."

I took one last look at her, then turned and left. Mandla followed, and offered to drive me home.

"I don't understand what she sees in him," I said as we drove through Joburg. "I know I'm not perfect but he's a monster!"

Mandla looked at me in surprise. "You don't really think she loves him, do you?"

"Doesn't she?"

He shook his head. "Jasper worked his way up the corporate ladder and got her father's attention. When he first started at Amazi he was Gideon's golden boy. Gideon loves him like a son and kept dropping hints, so she went out with him to make her father happy. Jasper is persistent when he wants something, and he wanted Ayanda. And she would do anything for her father."

I shuddered. "Even marry Jasper?"

"Unfortunately, yes."

*

Mandla was right. Six weeks later Vusi told me he had heard on the news that Ayanda and Jasper were engaged.

"She's not worth the tears, bra," he said, as we sat sipping beers in the shebeen.

"I'm not crying."

"You know what I mean."

We had finally hung up the dreadlock wig and shades for good. As far as our old clients were concerned, Prophet Mazinga had lost his powers and gone home to Mozambique. It made no difference to them. Within a few days they had all found someone new to give their money to.

Now we were calling ourselves "consultants", helping people track down wayward lovers, running errands, spying on cheating spouses. It was tacky, but at least it was honest. That was progress. Vusi had also managed to get a few shifts working as a security guard, and hoped to be able to make things legal with Zanele soon. It had been a rough few months, but we were survivors.

"Oh, no," Vusi muttered. "Trouble is coming this way."

I looked up to see Sweets moving towards us. I had never confronted her about ratting me out to Jasper and I had no desire to do so now. The past was the past.

"Hey boys," she said, squeezing in between us. She carried a newspaper and opened it on the table. "Did you hear the news? A big fancy engagement. Gideon Zwane's kid."

I couldn't help myself; I looked. There was a photo of Ayanda and Jasper at some event. She looked beautiful, but she didn't look happy. Jasper, on the other hand, was grinning from ear to ear. Soon he would have everything he wanted. The thought made me sick.

"Pretty girl, neh?" Sweets went on. "She would be a beautiful bride. Too bad the wedding is never going to happen."

I stared at her. "What's that supposed to mean? It says right here..."

"This paper is from last week," she said with a sly smile. "Things change."

I looked at her for a long time. "I know you were the one who told Jasper about the Prophet Mazinga scam, Sweets. You've hated me ever since...since things didn't work out with us."

Her smile faded. "So? He wanted answers and he was willing to pay for them."

"I knew it!" I gave her a dirty look. "How could you stab me in the back like that over something that happened so long ago?"

"Why are you surprised?" asked Vusi. "Everyone knows this woman is nothing but trouble."

"Hey, shut up!" Sweets snapped.

"He's right." I clicked my tongue in annoyance. "Ag, I shouldn't even be wasting my time talking to you. Why don't you go screw up someone else's life and leave me alone?"

"Are you joking?" She looked at me, shaking her head. "You ungrateful bastard."

"Ungrateful?" I let out a bitter laugh. "Am I supposed to thank you?"

"Hey wena, the wedding is off. You think that happened by magic?" She shoved me, knocking over my bottle.

I picked it up quickly before any of the beer could spill. "What the hell was that?" I stared at her, furious.

"That fool Jasper never paid me!" she yelled. "He wouldn't even answer when I called. Thank God I had everything on tape so I could give the bastard what he deserved. And after I got him out of the way, this is how you talk to me? Mxm! You men are all the same."

I was about to start a tirade of my own when something clicked. "Tape? What tape?"

"I recorded everything he said when we were together," she barked impatiently. "I'm not stupid. When he refused to pay I dropped off the tape at his girlfriend's place so she can see what a loser he is. Yoh, that fool can talk. A few drinks and he told me all about his big plan to marry Ayanda Zwane and steal her father's company, and how many times he cheated on her, and how he's been stealing money from right under her father's nose. There's no way she's going to marry him now. She's all yours thanks to me. So you better start showing me some respect!"

I was too stunned to reply. I looked at Vusi. Judging from the way his mouth was hanging open, I guessed he was also speechless.

"You recorded Jasper?" I asked finally.

Sweets rolled her eyes. "Isn't that what I just said?"

"And then you gave the tape to Ayanda?"

"Ja, I left it in her mailbox."

I licked my lips, still in shock. I didn't know what to think. I was relieved that Ayanda would finally know the truth about the man she wanted to marry, but none of that changed what had happened between us. I had lied to her and she would never forgive me.

"Sit down," I said to Sweets, feeling a little guilty about the way I had spoken to her. "Let me buy you a drink."

"A drink?" she shrieked. "You think a drink is going to fix the way you and your stupid friend talk to me? I don't want your drink. Just know that you owe me." She reached out and knocked over my bottle again, then shook her head and walked away.

I leapt to my feet as the puddle of beer poured over the side of the table and onto my lap. It reminded me of the champagne that had spilled on Jasper's pants at the charity event. What goes around comes around, I guess. All my scheming had achieved nothing. Even if Ayanda dumped Jasper, at that moment I was alone, broke and miserable, and I had no one to blame but myself.

*

I kept going to the orphanage, always making sure I was there during the week so I wouldn't run into Ayanda. One day, about a week after my run-in with Sweets, I went to Mother Superior. She looked at me with those kind eyes of hers, the eyes that had always seen through my silly stories and bravado.

"This is about your mother, isn't it?" she asked me. "You're finally ready to know who she is."

I nodded. It had been a long and painful process but I had decided that it was better to know the truth. "I need answers," I told Mother Superior. "I can't spend the rest of my life trying to fill in the blanks on my own."

"She was fourteen when she had you," she said in a soft voice. "Can you imagine? Still a child herself. And your father was...older. Much older, and married. The whole thing was..." She shook her head. "He wanted her to have an abortion, but even though she made mistakes she was a religious girl. She refused. He tried to force her. He...beat her. She came here to hide from him. It was the only place she would be safe. After a few months he moved away with his family. I heard that he died some time later. By the time your mother was ready to give birth, we all knew there was no way she could manage on her own, so we took you."

I didn't know what to say. I gritted my teeth with anger at the thought that a grown man could treat a young girl that way, after taking advantage of her. But I knew there was nothing I could do to change it. My father was gone now. It was over.

Mother Superior sighed. "You probably know her already. She's made quite a name for herself in the township. I'm sure you must have crossed paths with her once, maybe even many times."

I nodded. I had considered that possibility myself. It was strange think that the woman who gave birth to me might have sat next to me in a taxi, or passed me in the street. We might even have exchanged words without knowing it.

I looked at Mother Superior. "Tell me. Who is she?"

She hesitated, but only for a moment. "Her name is Thandi Mabizela."

I frowned. "I don't know anyone by that name."

"That's because everyone calls her by her nickname. Big Mama. She runs that big shebeen–"

"I know it." My head was spinning. Big Mama! No, there had to be a mistake. "Mother Superior, are you sure it's her?"

"Absolutely. In fact she came to see me a few months ago. Somehow she knew that you were planning to come and volunteer here, and she wanted to know if I was going to tell you about her."

For a minute I thought I had to be dreaming. Big Mama. I thought about all the time we had spent together over the years, the way she had taken me in and let me sleep in her shop, and all the times she gave me advice and let me buy beer on credit. I had always felt connected to her. One time, when I was still a kid, I asked why she didn't have any children. She never answered me. She just changed the subject.

"What did you say?" I asked Mother Superior.

"I told her I had every intention of telling you the truth. She didn't seem happy about it, but she accepted it. I haven't spoken to her since then."

I remembered the day I told Big Mama I was coming back to the orphanage. She had acted really weird, cutting off the conversation and rushing off. Now I knew why. She had come here to talk to Mother Superior. It was true, then. Big Mama was really my mother. I got to my feet and moved towards the door.

"Are you going to confront her?" asked Mother Superior.

"I have to," I said. I was surprised by how calm my voice sounded. "You don't understand – I know her. I've known her for years and she never said a word about this. I need an explanation!"

Mother Superior nodded. "I hope she can give you the answers you want."

I left the orphanage in a daze. My thoughts were spinning round and round. I couldn't believe it. No wonder Big Mama had been so maternal towards me all those years. And I had even told her she was like the mother I never had. I felt so stupid, so humiliated. She had made a complete fool of me! She got to have a relationship with her son while I was in the dark. How was that fair?

By the time I reached the shebeen I was really worked up. I barged in there and marched past the counter, ignoring the cashier, who was shouting that customers weren't allowed at the back. I opened the door and stepped into the office. Big Mama was sitting at the desk, checking the books. She looked up at me in shock, and then she sighed.

"She told you," she said.

"Yes. So it's true?"

Big Mama nodded. "I know how angry you must be, Senzo. If you want to shout at me, go ahead. Shout. I deserve it."

I opened my mouth, but nothing came out. I didn't tell her how hurt I was that she didn't want to raise me, or how angry I was that she had kept the secret for so long. I didn't tell her how betrayed I felt, or how much I had longed for a mother when I was small. I was tired. So much had happened over the last few months. I had found Ayanda and then lost her. I had learned that I wasn't an orphan, then found out my mother was the woman who owned the shebeen that was like my second home. I had gone from being a cocky hustler to being...I didn't know what I was anymore. I didn't know where my life was heading, and I was fed up with all of it.

I looked at Big Mama for a long time. I looked at her round shoulders and big eyes, the doek on her head, the way her fingers shook slightly on top of the desk. I thought about the story Mother Superior had told me, about everything Big Mama went through to protect me. I didn't know what she had felt the day she decided to give me up, but I knew that she must have loved me. When I left the orphanage she had given me a place to sleep. Maybe it was cowardly of her not to tell me the truth, but in her own way she had reached out. She had tried. She had done her best.

I couldn't shout at her. I couldn't be angry anymore, but I couldn't act like nothing had happened, either. I didn't know what to say, or how to act. So I did the only thing I could at that moment. I left.

*

For the next two days I went over every major decision I had ever made, trying to see where I went wrong. My life was a mess! The nuns had always tried to teach us to be kind and selfless. They talked about love a lot, but I was too bitter to listen. On the outside I had been a happy, mischievous kid, but on the inside I was angry and hurt. I didn't think anyone cared about me, so I decided to care about myself. I put my interests first. I tricked and cheated and lied because I thought there was no other way, but I was wrong.

Vusi came home with Zanele on the second night. She had brought big dishes of home-cooked food.

"You can't keep living on chips and vetkoek," she said, dishing out for us.

"We can't afford proper food," I told her. "We're honest men now, so we're going to be broke until this consultant thing works out."

"Lucky for you, I'm a good cook," she replied.

We sat down to eat, and Vusi started telling us about something funny that had happened during his security shift. Zanele listened attentively, even though I was sure she had already heard the story on the way to the flat. She even laughed at all the right moments. When his plate was empty, she dished another helping for him, and then another for me as well.

As I watched the two of them, I got the strangest feeling. It was like I had been walking around with a hood over my head and now I could finally see properly. Man, I had been so wrong. About Zanele, about love, about everything.

Zanele didn't piss me off because she was always interfering in my business. She pissed me off because I was jealous of her relationship with Vusi. For so long we were both losers, and then she came along and suddenly he was more than a stupid kid. He was a man with goals, with a plan, with something worth fighting for. And it drove me nuts. All this time I had chosen to see the woman who caused the change as a thorn in my side, when I should have seen her as the woman who helped my buddy grow up.

Vusi and Zanele loved each other. The real thing, deep and true and probably for a lifetime, the thing all the songs and movies talked about. They always put each other first. Zanele made Vusi think twice about the dumb stuff we did. She made him want to be better. I could see it so clearly then that I was amazed it had taken me so long.

That was what love looked like. Two people who gave themselves to the relationship completely, flaws and everything, people who trusted each other no matter what. Zanele and Vusi had the same goal – to make the other person happy. What I had been trying to build with Ayanda wasn't love at all. I had deprived her of the one thing she truly wanted – trust. How could I say I loved her?

Most of all I had been wrong about myself. I had tried to make myself into a fake hero for Ayanda and even with all the lies I managed to convince myself I was the good guy in this story. I was the one who could love her best. I was better than Jasper. But maybe I wasn't. I might not have cheated on her or tried to steal her father's company, but I betrayed her just as much as he did.

I felt the weight of hopelessness as I sat thinking about all of this. If only I had seen the truth sooner, I might have done things differently. It was too late now. There was nothing I could do to change what had happened with Ayanda, and I had to accept it and move on.

I couldn't give back the money I had taken from all those Prophet Mazinga clients, or take back all the lies I had told. But there was one relationship in my life I could still fix.

I picked up the dirty dishes, washed them and left them in a plastic bag for Zanele to take back with her, then I crept out of the flat. The two lovebirds didn't even notice. They were curled up on Vusi's mattress, talking in whispers.

I took a long walk to the shebeen. Big Mama was behind the counter, chatting loudly to one of the customers. I sat down in a corner and waited patiently for her to finish.

Finally she came over to me. "Hello, Senzo."

"Hi."

"What are you drinking? The usual?"

I shook my head. "I came because...if you're not busy...maybe we can talk."

She smiled. "Okay."

When she sat down beside me, I saw tears in her eyes.

*

Two months later I was walking around town, putting up new flyers. SV Consultants didn't have the same esoteric ring to it as Prophet Mazinga, but if I was going legit I had to do it properly. Me and Vusi had managed to get our company registered, with a little help from Big Mama. She had also lent us the start-up capital. Actually she handed me an envelope filled with cash, like some gangster. I refused to take it until she agreed to let me pay her back. Vusi said I should just call her Mama, but I had been calling her Big Mama for so long nothing else sounded right.

SV Consultants specialised in pretty much everything under the sun. We had expanded to company registration, permits, CVs and business plans, but we still tracked down runaway kids and cheating lovers. We were kasi boys, after all. We had to give our people what they wanted. We used the same space we had used for the consulting room, and once in a while someone would show up asking for Prophet Mazinga and we would have to deliver the unfortunate news that he was gone for good.

I walked up the steps to the office. When I stepped inside I saw the last person I had ever expected to see again. Ayanda. She sat in the chair opposite Vusi.

"Ah, there he is," said Vusi. "Told you he'd be back just now."

Ayanda turned around and our eyes met. My heart pounded. What was she doing here? How had she found me? More importantly, why was she looking for me?

"Hi Senzo," she said softly.

"Hi." I looked at Vusi, but he just wriggled his eyebrows and left us alone, mumbling some excuse about office supplies. "Ayanda, what are you doing here?"

"I heard Prophet Mazinga lost his powers," she said, standing up.

"Yes. It was for the best."

"I agree." She looked around the office. "This is a decent space. Congratulations."

"Thanks." I cleared my throat. "I heard about Jasper."

"Of course you did," she replied. There was a bitter note in her voice, and I didn't blame her. "When the marketing manager of one of the biggest companies in the country is arrested for fraud and embezzlement, it's going to make the news."

"Sorry."

She shrugged. "I should have known better than to trust him."

There was an awkward silence. "Ayanda, why are you here?"

She looked at me. "I couldn't stop thinking about you."

I stared at her in shock. "But..."

"I know," she sighed, then laughed. "You lied to me, made a fool of me, broke my trust. But for some reason I still believe you're a good person."

She opened her handbag and took out an old piece of folded paper. I knew what it was even before she opened it to reveal the poem written on the lined page.

"I wanted you to be the Senzo who wrote this," she whispered, "but I wasn't sure. Even after your crazy confession in my apartment, I wasn't sure. Then Nomfundo told me you knew the poem off by heart, and after that I couldn't get you out of my mind. I knew I had to see you again. I mean, what were the chances, right? It was like...destiny, or something."

I couldn't believe what I was hearing. No, I was afraid to believe it in case it was a dream. It had to be a dream. I had made a complete mess of things and there was no way Ayanda would forgive me in real life. Right?

She laughed nervously. "I must sound like a crazy person."

"No, I don't think you're crazy at all," I said hastily. "I know exactly what you mean."

"Do you?" She took a step towards me. "What I'm saying is I've come back. If you'll have me."

If? Was she crazy? She was all I had wanted since I was fourteen years old! But...

"I'm nobody," I reminded her. "I'm a broke false prophet who grew up in an orphanage. I'm a consultant who writes CVs for people and finds out if their husbands are cheating."

She took another step towards me. "I don't care."

I hesitated. "I'm trying to be a better person, but you know what they say – a prophet can't heal himself."

"You're not a prophet," she reminded me with a little laugh.

She leaned closer. I inched towards her... And then she kissed me. Man, that kiss had been a long time coming. Fifteen years, to be exact. I wrapped my arms around her waist and she wrapped hers around my neck. This time no one interrupted. There was no Jasper to pop up in his designer undies, waving old newspapers at us. The past was the past. This was a new beginning.

So you see, if you want to get the measure of a man, especially a complicated, imperfect, all too human citizen like myself, you have to understand what motivates him. For some men it's wealth or power. For me, it started with the fantasy of love, and grew into the real thing. It took a while to get there, but what can I say? Better late than never.

THE END

DID YOU KNOW?

Did you know that the best gift you could ever give an author is a review? It's easy to write one. Can I tell you how? Just mention one emotion you felt while reading, one thing you enjoyed or did not about the story, and whether you think others should read it or not. Yup! That's all. You can leave your review on the Amazon page where you bought this book. If you're reading off a computer, phone or tablet, here's the link:

https://www.amazon.com/dp/B07Y4W2T3V?ref_=pe_3052080_276849420

Thank you!

GET A FREE BOOK!

Would you like a FREE COPY of one of my upcoming novels? Click on this link (https://www.fidelnamisi.com/free-books), type your name and email address, and enter the draw for your chance to win.

GOOD LUCK!

Made in the USA
Coppell, TX
21 June 2021